WHITEWATER
SCRUBS

BY
JAMIE McEWAN

ILLUSTRATIONS BY JOHN MARGESON

DARBY
CREEK
PUBLISHING

To Thomas Edmund McEwan

Text copyright © 2005 by Jamie McEwan
Illustrations by John Margeson © 2005 by Darby Creek Publishing

Cataloging-in-Publication

McEwan, James.
Whitewater scrubs / by Jamie McEwan.
      p. ; cm.
ISBN-13: 978-1-58196-038-7
ISBN-10: 1-58196-038-7
Summary: Spring is in the air, and Clara has joined the "Scrubs" as they take up whitewater kayaking.
Usually she's one of the star athletes, but the whitewater has her scared!
1. Middle school students—Juvenile fiction. 2. Athletes—Juvenile fiction. 3. Kayaking—Juvenile fiction.
4. Self-perception—Juvenile fiction. [1. Middle school students—Fiction. 2. Athletes—Fiction. 3. Kayaks
and kayaking—Fiction. 4. Self-perception—Fiction.] I. Title.
PZ7.M478463 Wh 2005
[Fic] dc22
OCLC: 57625141

Published by Darby Creek Publishing,
A division of Oxford Resources, Inc.
7858 Industrial Parkway
Plain City, OH 43064
www.darbycreekpublishing.com

Printed in the United States of America

2 4 6 8 10 9 7 5 3 1

1-58196-038-7

CONTENTS

CHAPTER 1

TOO COOL FOR COMFORT

Clara sat in her kayak, blowing on her hands to warm them and wondering how she had let herself get talked into doing this stupid sport.

She was okay where she was, sitting in the calm water near the riverbank. But only ten yards away, the river was rushing by with a growling sound.

Out there in the current, the water was kicking up into waves. Ms. Parker, the instructor, was surfing the waves, going back and forth.

Fun for Ms. Parker, maybe.

But soon Clara would have to go out there.

She didn't want to.

It was early spring. The trees were still bare of leaves. The air was still chilly. The water was still freezing. It was too cold to be kayaking.

Clara looked at the others. Willy and Dan and Rufus were all bobbing in the eddy beside her.

It's all Willy's fault, thought Clara. *He's the one who said it would be cool to go kayaking every day instead of going out for a school sport.*

"I didn't know we had to do rapids," said Clara softly.

"That's what it's all about!" said Willy. "The Scrubs take on the wild river!"

"Yeah! Isn't this cool?" said Dan.

"No, it's not cool," said Rufus. "It makes me nervous. Doesn't it make you nervous?"

"Yeah," said Willy.

"Nah," said Dan. Dan was the smallest kid in the class, even smaller than Willy. But Dan wasn't afraid of anything.

Clara didn't say another word. She was afraid that if she talked, they might be able to tell how she felt.

Because Clara wasn't just nervous. She was really, really scared.

CHAPTER 2

WIDEST EYES

Until today, they had only paddled their kayaks on a pond. They had learned how to paddle in a straight line, how to turn, and how to lean their kayaks on their sides. Clara had done fine on the pond. But this was different.

"I should have gone out for lacrosse,"

said Clara. Willy gave her a funny look, so she didn't say anything more. But she couldn't help thinking how nice and dry and not scary playing lacrosse would be.

"Okay, Willy, it's your turn," said Ms. Parker as she came into the eddy alongside them. "Paddle out there into the current, go straight down the little drop, and then turn into the eddy on the right. Got it?"

Taking a deep breath, Willy nodded and started paddling.

"Remember to lean downstream!" called Ms. Parker. "Lean hard! Paddle! Keep paddling! Yeah! Way to go!"

Willy's kayak plunged over the drop and pitched up and down in the waves. Then he turned it into the calm water near shore. Willy looked back up at Clara, Dan, and Rufus and raised his paddle in the air.

"Yee-ha! Come on down, guys! It's great!" called Willy.

Dan's turn was next. He paddled hard. He was so light that he seemed to float over the waves. Dan made it look easy.

Then Rufus started paddling.

Rufus was big and strong, but he wasn't a tough guy. He was more like a really big teddy bear. And right now he looked too big for his kayak.

And he looked nervous.

Just as Rufus got to the current, he stopped paddling. The current caught him, and he slowly fell over.

Bloop! Rufus disappeared.

For a couple of seconds, there was no Rufus to be seen—just the bottom of his boat floating along in the current. Then his head popped up out of the water. He had come out of his boat. Rufus was coughing and had the widest eyes Clara had ever seen.

Right away, Ms. Parker was beside him. "Hold on!" she shouted. "Grab my boat!"

Ms. Parker paddled Rufus and his kayak to shore.

Clara was the only one left in the eddy.

She started breathing hard.

She couldn't believe she was really going to do this.

CHAPTER 3
SPLASH!

"All right, Clara!" called Ms. Parker from below. "Come on down!"

Clara bit her lip.

"Come on, Clara!" shouted Willy.

Soon they were all shouting encouragement—even Rufus, who was dripping wet and standing on the bank.

"You can do it! Yay, Clara!"

"I can't," said Clara softly. She knew that no one could hear her over the sound of the water. "I just can't."

"Go for it!" shouted Willy.

Clara had always been a good athlete— better than Willy, better than any of the others. Willy, Rufus, and Dan had all been third-string on the football team. Scrubs, people called them. Clara had been first-string in both soccer and basketball. She had won the last basketball game of the season by sinking a basket with only three seconds left on the clock.

Clara was sure that anything Willy could do, she could do better. Right? Right.

Maybe.

Now her friends were chanting. "Let's go, Clara, let's go! Let's go, Clara, let's go!"

Clara put her paddle into the water and pulled, first on one side of the kayak, then on the other.

She paddled into the current and turned downstream. The water just ahead was smooth and green, but then it fell over a little hump and turned bubbly and white. Waves slammed into each other like rowdy kids in the crowded hallways at school.

As Clara paddled over the drop, she felt her kayak tilt forward. Here came the first wave. It splashed her right in the face. She blinked and lost her balance. She caught one glimpse of Willy's face looking right at her, and then . . .

SPLASH!

She was upside-down. All around her was dark water, and Clara couldn't see anything. She couldn't breathe. And the water was cold!

Clara struggled, she kicked, but for one terrifying moment she couldn't get out of her kayak. Then she remembered that she had to pull off the spray skirt to get out. She found the handle, pulled it, pushed herself out, and swam to the surface. She took a big, full breath of air.

"Grab on!" said Ms. Parker.

Clara grabbed on to Ms. Parker's loop pole and was pulled to shore.

CHAPTER 4

WHITEWATER WIMP

Clara went home mad. Her feet were cold, her hair was wet, and she was mad.

She didn't really know what she was mad *at*. She was just mad.

Mad at herself, maybe.

"So how was paddling today?" asked

Clara's mother at dinner.

Clara hesitated. She wanted to tell someone about it, but she also didn't want to sound like a wimp. Not even to her mother. And especially not to her little brother, Derek.

"It was fine," said Clara finally.

"Are you sure?" her mom asked. "You sound a little . . . something."

"Yeah, it was fine."

"Your hair is wet," said Derek.

"Well, okay, I tipped over, and I got wet. But that was cool."

"I bet it was *cold*," said Derek.

"Yeah," said Clara. "That, too. But no problem."

"It's no problem to tip over?" her mother asked.

"Not really. Lots of people tip over. Ms. Parker says it's part of the learning process."

That was easy for Ms. Parker to say. Ms. Parker knew how to roll her kayak. She could tip over upside-down, and then, with a stroke of her paddle, she could bring the boat right-side-up again. Ms. Parker said she was going to teach them all how to roll when the water got warmer.

That didn't help Clara today.

All the next day Clara had a weird feeling in the pit of her stomach, as if she had swallowed a baseball. And every time she thought of kayaking that afternoon, the ball got heavier.

It was like a ball of lead by the time she was riding in the van to the river. It made it hard for her to breathe.

The three boys didn't seem scared. They were talking and joking like always. Clara stared out the window and watched the trees go by. All too soon she saw the river.

She wanted to quit, right then and there. But what would she do? Sit in the van? What would the guys say? She sighed and put on her helmet and lifejacket.

But when she got out and looked out at the rapid, Clara almost choked from fear.

"Ms. Parker?" Clara said. "I don't want to go in the water today. I have a sore throat, and my mom said maybe I shouldn't get wet."

"I'm sorry you're not feeling well," said Ms. Parker. "Why don't you and Rufus just paddle on the flatwater? That way you won't get wet. And Rufus can use the practice."

Immediately Clara felt better. The weight in her belly was gone. It was only the rapids that made her feel so afraid.

But when Clara went home, she felt bad that she had lied to Ms. Parker. She wanted to tell her mom about it. But she just couldn't tell anyone that she'd been afraid and that she had lied. So she didn't say anything.

She didn't want to admit she had been a wimp.

Which, Clara realized, made her even *more* of a wimp.

CHAPTER 5

NOTHING TO PROVE

The next morning Clara had that funny feeling in her stomach again.

She decided she had to tell somebody. So at recess she caught Julie, just as Julie was coming out of the school doors.

"Can I talk to you, Julie?"

"Sure, what's up?"

Julie wore jeans like Clara, was tall like Clara, and played all kinds of sports like Clara. She was the perfect person for Clara to talk to. They had been friends since they were little kids. Last fall they had been on the soccer team together. And Julie was the kind of person who never seemed worried about anything.

"It's about this kayaking stuff," began Clara. Then Clara told Julie how she had tipped over and how scared she'd been and how she had lied about having a sore throat. "And now I'm scared all over again," Clara finished.

"So why don't you just quit?" asked Julie.

"Well, you know," said Clara. But Julie just looked puzzled, so Clara had to go on. "It would be chicken to quit."

"Nobody'd know that, though," said Julie. "Besides, nobody cares about kayaking. It's a dumb sport. The only guys doing it are the Scrubs. Nobody cares what *they* think."

"I care what they think," said Clara. "Besides, *I* would know!"

"So what?"

Clara was surprised. She had expected Julie to tell her to keep going, tough it out, hang in there, you can do it. Or maybe Clara had *wanted* her to say that.

"You really think I should just quit?" asked Clara.

"Absolutely," said Julie. "You've been first-string on two teams already. Time to take it easy. You've got nothing to prove."

Clara frowned.

"You don't want to hang around with those losers anyway," said Julie.

"Hey, they're not losers!" said Clara.

"Yeah they are," said Julie. "Look at them."

Clara looked over. Rufus had just made some joke, and Dan and Willy were bent over with laughter.

"They're so *immature*," said Julie.

Clara thought about it all afternoon, all through classes. Julie's advice made sense. Why not quit?

But Clara didn't feel any more comfortable about quitting than she did about being underwater. Clara remembered reading an interview with a star soccer player who'd said, "I never quit. I just never quit."

Clara thought that was an awfully cool thing to say. She wanted to be like that, too. Why was it so hard to make up her mind?

Clara decided to use the sore throat excuse one more time.

So she paddled flatwater with Rufus again.

Rufus was still having a hard time paddling in a straight line. Clara cruised around with him. They talked about basketball and wrestling and the Mets versus the Yankees. Rufus knew his sports.

It was actually kind of fun.

But Clara knew she was going to have to go back into the rapids sometime.

Or quit.

CHAPTER 6
COLD AND STUFF

That Sunday Clara sat in her bedroom and made a list. Her mom always did that when she had to decide something. There were lists all over the house.

When Clara finished, her list looked like this:

Quit	Don't Quit
Dry! Warm!	Prove that I can take it.
Won't have to be bad.	Might get better.
Be friends with cool people.	Stay friends with the Scrubs.

There was another problem that didn't seem to fit under either column. It really bugged her that she was worse at kayaking than Willy and Dan. It seemed unfair. Clara had always been good at everything. Quitting wouldn't make her any better, but if she quit, she wouldn't have to be reminded all the time that they were better.

Making the lists didn't help her. Both sides balanced out. So what should she do?

She went to bed that night sure she should keep kayaking.

She woke up in the morning sure she should quit.

"Hey, Mom," Clara asked at breakfast, "is it okay for me to quit kayaking if I want to?"

"Why would you want to?" her mom asked.

"I don't know. It's just cold. And it takes a lot of time. And stuff."

"And stuff?" asked Derek.

"Yeah, stuff."

"You can quit if you really want to," said her mother. "If you're sure."

Clara thought she was sure.

CHAPTER 7
YARD SALE

She stayed sure until school was over and she walked to the parking lot. That's when she should have told Ms. Parker she wasn't going. Instead she got in the van. It was just easier.

"There's always room for Jell-O!" shouted Rufus as he piled in last. Rufus said that almost every afternoon. Dan punched Rufus in the arm, and Rufus gave Dan a noogie, and they all laughed. Clara laughed with them.

When they got to the river, they put all their gear on. Wearing helmets and life-jackets and spray skirts and carrying their paddles, they looked ridiculous, like some alien life forms. How, Clara wondered, did she ever get involved in this freaky sport?

It was a bright, sunny day, but that didn't make it much warmer. They drove to a new place on the river to run some differ-ent rapids.

"Clara," said Ms. Parker, "you and Rufus aren't quite ready for this first rapid. I'll put you in the pool at the bottom. We'll paddle down to you, and then we'll all paddle down the easier rapids together."

So Clara and Rufus sat in the pool at the bottom of the rapid to watch the others.

Willy came down first. For a while Willy was doing fine, but as he got near the end of the rapid, he headed straight for a rock.

"Willy! Look out! Look out!" shouted Clara.

It was too late. Willy tried to turn, but he bumped the rock anyway. It tipped him right over.

And then Dan, who had been following Willy, ran into Willy's boat. Dan tipped over, too.

In an instant paddles and boats and kids were everywhere.

"Yard sale!" said Rufus. That's what they called it when equipment got scattered all over. "Yard sale!"

Clara wasn't laughing.

The Whitewater Scrubs were in big trouble!

CHAPTER 8
KICK!

"Clara! Rufus!" Ms. Parker shouted as she paddled toward them. "You get Willy! I'll get Dan! Go!"

Rufus was closer. He tried to paddle out into the current, but he got swept downstream, back into the pool. Clara did better. She paddled up beside Willy's boat, but

Willy was on the other side of his boat, away from her.

"Grab onto my boat!" yelled Clara.

Willy looked scared. He just floated there, his head bobbing up and down in the waves. Clara paddled around his kayak and got right next to him.

"Okay, take it! Hold on!" shouted Clara again.

Finally Willy grabbed hold.

"Don't worry about his boat," called Ms. Parker from upstream. Dan was holding onto the back of her boat. "Just get Willy in."

Clara paddled hard, but Willy was heavy. Clara thought she'd never get to shore. "Kick your feet!" she shouted to Willy. "Kick!"

Willy kicked, and at last Clara managed to tow him to shore. Dan was already there.

Afterwards, it took Ms. Parker a long time to rescue the kayaks. Willy and Dan were really cold, so none of them did any more paddling. Everyone packed up to go home.

Willy and Dan shivered all the way back.

"How about today?" Willy asked Dan as they rode. "Weren't you scared when you swam out today?"

"Nah," said Dan. "Little guys can't afford to get scared."

Rufus looked at Clara. "Aren't you glad we're allowed to be scared?" Rufus asked her.

"She's not scared," said Willy. "I'm the one who's scared."

"You know, it's good to be scared," said Rufus. "That shows you're still sane."

"What fun is that?" asked Dan.

Clara didn't say anything. But she agreed with Rufus.

CHAPTER 9

BEING A SCRUB

The next day at recess Willy came up to Clara.

"Thanks again, for rescuing me," he said.

"My pleasure," said Clara. Which was true. It had been fun to help somebody out. It made her feel important.

"I wanted to tell you," said Willy, "I'm going to quit. I'm not going out this afternoon."

"Why not?" Clara was really surprised.

"I have never been so scared in my life," said Willy. "I don't think I'll ever get in a kayak again."

Clara was about to say something, but she stopped because it occurred to her that if Willy didn't paddle anymore, but she did, then she would be better than Willy at everything. Which was the way it should be.

But she felt sure that Willy shouldn't

quit. This was Willy's chance to be good at something. She couldn't let him miss it. So Clara went ahead and said, "You know, that's exactly the way I felt the first time I swam out."

"You? I don't believe it."

"Oh, yeah, me. You know those days I said I had a sore throat? I was lying. I wasn't sick. I was just scared."

"I didn't think you were scared of anything," said Willy.

"Well, I am. Yesterday I was sure I was going to quit. I just thought I'd come out one last time."

"Maybe we should both quit," said Willy.

"You can't quit!" said Clara. "You're really good at it! You're so much better than I am. You're a natural. It'll be warmer soon, and you'll learn how to roll, and you'll look back and laugh at what happened yesterday. I'm the one who's going to quit, because I'm so bad at it. But you're really, really good."

"You're not so bad," said Willy.

"I'm bad compared to you."

"You're just tippy."

"I'm bad. I'm a . . . ," she hesitated.

"A Scrub?" asked Willy.

"Yeah," said Clara.

"Is that such a bad thing?" asked Willy.

Clara felt embarrassed. Willy and Rufus and Dan always acted like they were proud of being Scrubs.

"I'm not used to being bad at things," said Clara.

"It's not so terrible," said Willy. "You can be bad and still have fun."

Clara didn't say anything. She looked across the schoolyard. Julie was looking over at them. What would Julie think? Clara wondered. What would all her team-mates think?

"Listen," said Willy, "I'll keep kayaking if you do."

"You have to keep kayaking," said Clara.

"I'll do it if you do it," he said. "Just think—I might need you to rescue me again.

"Okay," said Clara. "Okay, I'll try. I guess I can stand being a Scrub."

CHAPTER 10

RACE DAY

The Riverfest Slalom was held on a sunny afternoon in the middle of May. It was a beautiful day for a race.

Clara was waiting by the scoreboard or her score to be posted. She had finished her first run. Her clothes were wet from the waves splashing on her, but that didn't matter because it was so warm.

"Hey, Clara, how'd it go?" asked Willy.

"Okay. Pretty well. I made all the gates. How about you?"

"It was great," said Willy. "It was so much fun. I just hope I can have a good second run, too."

"Yeah, me, too."

"Hey, thanks for getting me to keep kayaking," said Willy.

"Well, thanks for getting me to stay, too," said Clara. "I'm glad I did."

They shook hands. Just then Rufus and Dan joined them.

"Hey, guys, the scores are up," said Dan. He turned to Willy: "You're ahead of me, you turkey. By a whole two seconds."

"Wow, that's close," said Willy.

"Pretty darned close," said Dan, grinning. "By the way, I'm standing third. You're second."

"You're kidding!" said Willy.

"Congratulations, you guys," said Clara.

"Congratulations right back at you," said Dan. "You're third in the junior women."

"I am?"

"You bet," said Dan.

"Yeah, but how about me?" said Rufus.

"Hey, you're in fifth so far. That isn't bad," said Dan.

"You don't *always* have to be the best of us," said Willy.

"I'm just happy I made it down the race course," said Rufus.

They shook hands all around. Clara could tell Rufus really was happy to have made it down the river without tipping over. They all were. Just finishing the course right-side-up was an accomplishment.

"Hey, good going, you guys," said a voice from behind.

They turned around. It was Julie and a whole group of other kids from school.

"That was really fun to watch," Julie went on. "I can't believe you guys could really do it."

"Do you still think this is a dumb sport?" Clara asked Julie.

Julie thought for a moment. "Now that it's a warm day," she said, "it doesn't look so dumb. But I still think it was dumb in March!"

Everybody laughed.

"Are you guys going to keep kayaking over the summer?" Julie asked.

"Maybe," said Willy. "We haven't talked about it."

"If you do, let me know," said Julie. "I might want to try it, too."

"What do *you* think, Clara?" asked Willy. "Are we going to sign up again?"

"I refuse to think about it," said Clara, "until I'm through with the race. One more run to go. Ask me after that."

CHAPTER 11

WET AND WILD

Clara was nearing the end of her second run. It was a good run. It was even better than her first run.

Don't mess up, she told herself as she paddled toward Gate 19.

Gate 19 was an upstream gate. Clara had

to go past it, turn around in the eddy behind it, and then paddle up through it. Then she had to paddle downstream through the last gate, Gate 20, and finally across the finish line.

Clara paddled through Gate 19. She leaned downstream so the current wouldn't tip her. Too far! She lost her balance and tipped over.

SPLASH! The water closed over her.

She couldn't breathe. She couldn't see. She almost panicked. But then she thought, *No, wait. I know what to do. I've practiced this.*

She reached her paddle way up above her, all the way to the surface. Then she pushed her head down and twisted her hips. All of a sudden the world was in its right place again. She had rolled her boat up! Right in the waves!

People on the bank cheered and shouted, "Go through Gate Twenty!"

The loudest voice of all was Ms. Parker's. "Look up! Gate Twenty!"

Clara shook her head and blinked the water from her eyes. She looked downstream. There was Gate 20. She could do it. She paddled over and through the gate. Then she glided over the finish line.

Clara raised the paddle over her head. "Yee-hah! I did it!" she yelled.

Over on the bank, the onlookers were still cheering. She paddled over to the crowd.

"Yay, Clara!" yelled Ms. Parker. Clara could hear her mother and her brother Derek cheering, too.

"Hey, do you get extra points for rolling?" shouted Derek.

Clara laughed and shook her head.

Dan and Willy came down and held her boat while Clara got out.

"That was so cool," said Dan.

"Way to go!" said Willy.

"Okay," said Clara with a grin. "*Now* let's talk about summer."

Drayton,
    Thanks for your
support.
        Best Wishes!

            Bob Little

CHASERS

An EMS Story

CHASERS
An EMS Story

A Novel by

Robert J. Little

Published by: Triple Earth Publishing LLC
                 10 Church Street – Box 815
                 Nanuet, New York 10954

First Edition: November 2014

Creative Editor: Michael H. Brown
Line Editor: Jason Kaplowitz
Cover Graphic Design by Belinda Hinds-Lewis
Author photograph by Robert Haig

The characters and events of this book are fictitious. Any similarity to real persons, living or dead, is entirely coincidental and not intended by the author.

ISBN 978-0-692-33768-4

Printed in the United States of America

DEDICATION AND THANKS

This book is dedicated to the memory of Helen Turnage. Grandma, who, with basically a fifth grade education, but a superior intellect and voracious appetite for knowledge, constantly encouraged me to read. She was an inspiration for writing this book.

Also, this book is dedicated to the memory of my son Richard "Rick" Little. Richard the Kindhearted/Richard the Lionhearted, who would give the coat off his back in the middle of a blizzard to help the very old and the very young. He was a major motivation in 'finishing' this book. His death at the age of 34 reminded me of the words that 'tomorrow is not promised,' and that 'one should never die with their dream/song in their heart.'

Thanks goes out to all the partners that I have worked with over my many years in the Emergency Medical Service field. My partners, the Good, the Bad and the Ugly, helped make me a better EMT/Medic and a better person. Many of you were great EMTs and Medics, but even more so, many of you were a class act and great human beings. Together, I like to think, we helped save countless lives and helped bring numerous precious new lives into this world. Sometimes we were considered heroes, but amongst each other we considered it just doing our job. We looked for nothing in return except the acknowledgement of a 'thank you', and we chuckled with pride, or embarrassment, whenever our deeds made the news. We usually didn't have the danger of dodging bullets, or going into burning buildings, but we had the danger of being exposed to every disease and illness known to man (most recently, the Dallas EMS crew that was exposed to the first case of Ebola in the U.S.) on a daily basis and the danger of job related accidents. My deepest sympathies go out to friends and families who lost loved ones in the line of duty or due to job-related contracted diseases.

Thanks to my family for their patience and encouragement. Thanks to "Professor" Mike for the education and Robyn for your ideas and input. Thanks to my second EMS family at Nanuet Ambulance Corps for their moral support.

Special thanks to Donovan and Diane. Donovan, for your unsolicited and unbounded support in so many ways. In a short period of time, I lost one son but gained another. I have to confess that, on many occasions, I tapped into that positive and dynamic energy that emanates from your soul. When I grow up, I want to be just like you. Diane, thanks for your love, support and encouragement, especially at the beginning of this writing. You brought so much to the table at that time and offered 200%, eagerly. Your insights, attention to detail and exceptional research skills, were a tremendous help for which I am eternally grateful.

CHAPTER

1

TWO YOUNG HISPANIC MALES flagged down one of the many 'gypsy' cabs speeding through the intersection at 149th Street and Southern Boulevard. It was a hot August night, but even at 1AM the streets of the South Bronx were alive with both, car and pedestrian traffic.

The summer heat had driven many of the South Bronx residents without portable air conditioners out of their sweltering concrete ovens and into the cooler night air. Many of the adults sat playing cards or dominoes on folding card chairs on the sidewalk with loud music blaring from stereo speakers placed in open apartment windows. Others sat on apartment building stairs or on the nearest parked cars, while their young children played in a running sprinkler system attached to a nearby fire hydrant. Even a few of the adults joined the children and cooled off by running through the sprinkler, their restraint discarded due to the repressive summer heat and the influence of beer and rum. A few of the women shrieked as they ran from the sudden coldness of the sprinkler water with their saturated, clinging tee shirts revealing bra-less breasts. The shrieking from the women momentarily diverted the attention of the men at the card game, who laughed at the women but kept an interested eye on the bouncing breasts underneath the wet tee shirts.

An old black Lincoln Town Car, the car of preference for 'gypsy' cab companies because of its size and elegance, pulled to a stop in front of the two men. The bright lights from the White Castle hamburger restaurant across the street illuminated the corner as the short stocky male with the New York Yankee tee shirt and baseball cap opened the rear passenger door and got in. The thin male with a large Puerto Rican flag printed on the chest of his white tee shirt got in behind him, closed the door and said, "Soundview and Bruckner, to the chicken joint on the corner."

The driver nodded, then repeated the location in a thick African accent and pulled off proceeding north on Southern Blvd. He thought, what a good night it had been so far. No one had jumped out without paying their fare and no one had wanted to curse and fight, feeling they had been cheated or overcharged. He made enough money to make this night a good money night if he stopped now, but the best part of the night was still ahead. The bars and clubs would be closing soon and usually that two or three-hour period was when he could double his take for the night.

After several blocks of rows of five story apartment buildings and small closed up store-fronts had passed, Yankee tee shirt and cap reached into his jogger's belt pouch and stealthily removed a small caliber gun. He looked at Puerto Rican shirt who nodded. Yankee shirt, who was sitting directly behind the driver waited until the driver stopped at a red light. He quickly reached through the open plexiglass partition and smacked the African against the temple, holding the gun there. "Listen muthafucka, give me all the money you got or I'll blow your brains into that bodega across the street...."

But, before he could get the full sentence out of his mouth, the African grabbed the pistol barrel with a huge strong hand, pointed it toward the passenger's side windshield, then he floored the gas pedal.

The Lincoln's powerful engine roared as the car took off like a rocket at a launching pad. With tires screeching it flew through the intersection as the life and death struggle ensued inside its cabin. Suddenly two shots rang out, followed by the loud screech of another car's tires and the impact of the second car slamming into the rear of the Lincoln as it passed through another intersection. The Lincoln was knocked onto the sidewalk striking a fire hydrant, a bus-stop pole, then hit a parked car and flipped over onto its top and skid for another twenty feet. The eerie sound of metal versus concrete pierced the night as the gypsy cab finally stopped ten feet away from the front of a social club, upside down on the sidewalk.

Some of the occupants and members of a store-front neighborhood social club, mainly teens and young adults, were standing outside smoking cigarettes, marijuana and drinking. Some heard the shots and collision, and ran over to the car to try to help. Others backed up and ran inside to tell others to call 9-1-1.

The African, dazed and momentarily disoriented, tried to gather himself. He hung there upside down in his cousin's cab for a long moment. He felt someone tugging at his sleeve, trying to pull him out and wondered 'could it be robbers? Was it neighborhood crack-heads trying to get his money?' He heard the voices of a gathering crowd outside the car and wondered if it was safe to get out. He released the seatbelt, crawled out through the driver's window over the broken glass and into the dimly lit street.

EMT Dexter Reed and his partner EMT Roman Reyes pulled to a halt in their South Bronx Emergency Care Services ambulance. Although it was almost one fifteen in the morning there were enough people and emergency services equipment arriving to light up the area like a major sports stadium, with more on the way. The Fire Department of New York protocol was usually to send two Engines, two Trucks and a Battalion Chief but with a person pinned inside the auto, the tally of vehicles would increase by a Rescue Unit and a Squad Unit.

The gypsy cab lay on its top with a just arriving New York City Fire Department crew stabilizing the unsteady car and trying to cut it open to get to the people inside. Some of the fire department crewmen were running toward the auto with heavy saws and long spear-like equipment.

Dexter saw a familiar face walking toward him. "Hey Dex-tahh. What's up with your Knicks? Looks like they are gonna suck again this year. You got the story on this?" asked the NYPD officer pointing to the overturned cab.

"Nah, Brian. We got it as an MVA with a possible pin job," said Dexter, as he and Roman pulled their equipment from the ambulance and readied it.

"Check this out. Two young punks get into this gypsy cab at 149th Street. They tell the cabbie to take them to the Soundview section of the Bronx. A few blocks later they try to stick him up at a red light. The cabbie grabs the gun and floors the gas pedal. Shots go off and then the cab gets hit by another car. The car hits a fire hydrant and a parked car then flips over."

"So what are we talking, maybe three bodies in the car?" asked Dexter.

"Naw, only one. Amazingly, the shooter got away but the second perp is unconscious and pinned in the back seat. FDNY is trying to cut his dumb ass out. The cab driver crawled out the window and is walking around somewhere... there he is, over there, sitting on the curb. Man, what a pair of balls," remarked the officer with admiration.

As the officer spoke, an ESU truck from NYPD rumbled onto the scene followed closely by a detective cars and a high-ranking NYPD official.

Dexter began walking toward the gypsy cab driver with a cervical collar and long spinal immobilization board, while transmitting a request over his portable EMS radio for a paramedic unit for the confirmed unconscious pin job. As Dexter spoke into his radio, he subconsciously compensated for the noise traffic he could hear behind and around him from the voices, radios and engines of the several different NYC agencies on the scene.

"Central, be advised, this is SoBro 1. We are going to need a medic unit at this scene. We have two patients from an overturned car with one patient still trapped inside the vehicle. At this time we are unable to determine the status of the trapped patient."

It didn't surprise Dexter that the cab driver was an African immigrant from Senegal who spoke with a thick African and French accent. Nine of every ten cabs in New York were driven by immigrants. Taxi driving was one of the few jobs open to new immigrants, who often find other jobs closed to them if they have accents or limited English skills and are not U.S. citizens. It was common to find African immigrants and recently transplanted natives from the Dominican Republic driving the cab service cars, or gypsy cabs, in the South Bronx. Whether due to economic or racial bias, the yellow medallion cabs from Manhattan didn't travel beyond the pricey, glitzy borders of the Upper East or West Sides of Manhattan. Going to Harlem, the Bronx or parts of Brooklyn were considered operating in treacherous waters to experienced, knowledgeable yellow cab drivers, hence the need for, and the thriving of, Car Service companies in the outer boroughs. No major training, skill or higher education was required, and since the money was cash-in hand, most drivers went home with an untaxed day's pay in their pocket.

In an area depicted by a recent U.S. Census as one of the poorest areas in the nation, cabs and grocery stores were the usual targets of the common robbers, thieves and junkies looking for a quick score. Cab drivers were aware of the obvious danger involved or perhaps were accustomed to such trauma and violence in their countries, where people frequently died from trauma and violence.

Dexter signaled to Roman, who was talking on his cell phone, that he was going to check out the cab driver. Roman nodded.

"Hello, sir. Are you hurt or in pain?" asked EMT Dexter as he observed the man sitting in front of him on the street curb. Instinctively, Dexter bent his six-foot tall frame over and knelt down on one knee facing the patient. This gesture put him on eye level with the patient to prevent him from arching his neck, and also gave the psychological effect of putting Dexter and patient on the same plane, calming the patient.

The flashing lights reflected off Dexter's young, oval brown face and doe eyes. A moustache, and sideburns that ended at the bottom of his ears, gracefully complimented his features and short hair. He presented a professional appearance and saw himself, in the near future, getting his bachelors' degree then applying for medical school. Not one for gaudiness, the only pieces of jewelry were a two hundred fifty dollar diver's watch and a thin gold necklace with a gold crucifix, both gifts.

"I am okay. I am fine, sir" replied the driver in a calm and collected voice.

"What is your name?"

"My name is Josef Mamadou Soumare."

"Do you remember what happened, Mr. Soumare?"

"Yes. Two young guys tried to rob my money and we crashed" said the Senegalese man.

"Mr. Soumare, I am with EMS. Do you mind if I ask you a few more questions and check out your injuries?"

A paramedic crew arrived just as the fire department and police got the cab cut open. With the help of Roman, a third ambulance crew and the special police unit, the medics did spinal immobilization, CPR and began administering drugs to the non-breathing patient. They then immediately transported him, radioing ahead to nearby Bronx Mercy Hospital to have a team of surgeons on standby awaiting them at the ER.

Dexter convinced their patient to go to the hospital for a precautionary check-up, and they proceeded to the hospital, with Roman driving.

"C'MON ROMIE, THEY'RE CALLING US FOR A JOB"
said Dexter to his partner, who was smoking a cigarette outside the ambulance.

"Callin who? We just came out the hospital after dropping the African off," reasoned Roman.

"Romie, you forget it's Saturday night? The bars and clubs are closing now, it's about to get busy. Besides, I think it's a full moon tonight."

"Damn, don't nobody stay home on Saturday nights and make babies anymore?" grumbled Roman as he flung his cigarette to the curb. A small figure emerged from the shadows, bent down, picked up the cigarette butt and examined it, startling Roman. "Damn it, Mary."

Mary paid Roman no mind, fully engrossed in examining the cigarette under the light of the hospital floodlights located twenty feet above the ground on the hospital walls. She then stepped back into the shadows of the night.

Mary was one of the hospital's resident homeless persons, who lived on the perimeter of the hospital's outer property borders for the past few years. She usually slept on cardboard, with rags or more cardboard as covers, on the hospital parking lots or grounds.

With lights and sirens blaring they arrived to find one of the two cars, an old two door Honda, laying on its passenger side on the sidewalk and up against the wall of a five story apartment building. A six-foot long scratch, the color of the silver from the auto's body, scarred the concrete pavement and left evidence of the violent skid-stop.

The other car, a five-year-old Cadillac, sat awkwardly pointing in the wrong direction with one of its wheels on the curb at the corner of the south Bronx intersection. Dexter and his partner Roman pulled to halt in their South Bronx Emergency Care Services Type-I ambulance. Although it was four in the early summer morning, a small curious crowd had started to gather around the perimeter of the accident scene. The NYC Fire Department had arrived first and the red and white flashing/revolving lights served as a beacon in the darkness. Strangely enough to Dexter, most of the Fire Department crew of about five men were gathered around the Cadillac and tending to its driver, a large black man, while the others hosed down the area around the accident. Dexter and Roman got out of their ambulance and quickly walked over to the driver of the Honda, a Mexican, who had climbed out of the car and sat on the sidewalk curb. He seemed either a little dazed or a little drunk. He responded to questions in Spanish from Roman, who took over the questioning of the driver for mental alertness and the extent of his injuries, while Dexter went over to the driver of the Cadillac. As Dexter observed the driver of the Cadillac, something seemed very odd to him. Four of the five-man-crew of the fire trucks, all Caucasian, were doing their best to treat the black driver of the Cadillac with care and attentiveness.

In New York City, the great 'melting pot', where the majority of the population of roughly eight million are ethnic minorities, it always baffled Dexter how a New York City agency like the New York Fire Department, in one of the largest northeastern cities in the United States could get away with de facto segregation in the twenty-first century. Dexter acknowledged the tremendous risks firefighters take and the bravery exemplified by them. He had no animosity toward the firefighters and didn't blame them, but how could a city agency in New York, not Alabama nor Mississippi, have the least diverse fire department of any major U.S. city? Dexter had read a recent newspaper report which revealed that the NYC Fire Department had roughly eleven thousand firemen of which nearly ninety percent were Caucasian males, four percent black and about seven percent Hispanic. In comparison, the NYC police department with approximately forty thousand police personnel had seventeen percent black and eighteen percent Latino. The City's Emergency Medical Service was nearly fifty percent minority.

Dexter stepped through the firemen until he was face to face with the driver of the Cadillac. A big, burly black man, dressed like he was coming from a party, with a powder blue dress shirt opened at the collar, gray sport-jacket and dark dress slacks sat on the bumper of the fire truck which was parked next to his Cadillac.

"Hello, sir. I'm with EMS. How are you feeling?" asked Dexter.

"I'm okay, but my car needs CPR and to be rushed into surgery," chuckled the driver after he exhibited a delay in focusing on Dexter's face.

"You are going to be okay, brother. We'll look after your car and you can give my men any of your personal belongings, we'll hold it at our station," said one of firemen identifying himself as the lieutenant of the fire crew. "He should go to the hospital. He's a little shook up."

Dexter, a five year EMT, prepped his patient before asking the standard questions to determine the driver's mental status. "Sir, please bear with me. I have to ask you a few questions to make sure you didn't hit your head and everything is working correctly, okay?"

"Sure, my man. Fire away," said the driver who seemed friendly and happy.

"First, let's start off with a simple one. What's your name?"

"Johnny Williams."

"What hurts you, Johnny?"

"I got a little headache."

"Do you know where you are?"

"Sure, I am in the Bronx, Hunts Point Avenue and Randall Avenue. But don't tell my wife. She thinks I'm at a union meeting in Westchester, if she finds out that I was at a topless bar, all hell will break loose," smiled the driver looking at the firemen and winking. They all laughed.

"Do you know what today is?" Dexter continued.

"Uh, today is Saturday."

"I need the date too."

"Oh. Uh, it's August 1, 2010."

"Think about that. Are you sure?"

The driver looked up at the firemen and could tell by their expressions that he was wrong. "Uh, August 2, 2010?"

"No, Mr. Williams, you are off on the year by a few. I think that you may have suffered a slight concussion and that you need to go with us to the hospital," said Dexter making a mental note of the alcohol he detected on the driver's breath.

"Listen brother, do what the paramedics say and go the hospital. We will take care of everything for you. Your car isn't drivable. We'll have it towed to the station and park it there. It will be safe. Give us your number and, if you want, we'll call your wife and tell her what happened, and doctor it up a little," said the fire lieutenant.

"Yeah, brother. We'll take care of everything. Just get yourself checked out," echoed another fireman.

"Alright, alright. I'm all yours, just be gentle with me," joked the driver toward Dexter.

Dexter explained to the driver the next steps and sequence of events leading up to the arrival at the hospital emergency room. Dexter then manually applied and held stabilization to the driver's neck, while he signaled Roman to get a cervical collar, long board and stretcher from the ambulance.

Although Roman took a little more time than usual before coming back with a stretcher, long-board and collar, Dexter, who was curious about Roman's behavior lately, dismissed it. While Roman was getting the equipment from the ambulance, Dexter considered calling the dispatcher over the radio to ask if there was another unit available for the transport of the second patient. He didn't think it was wise to transport both drivers in the same ambulance due to the potential for violent disagreement over who was wrong and caused the accident. But he reasoned that the two drivers had a language barrier and therefore the possibility of an argument or fight ensuing during the ride to the emergency room was slim. Plus the fact that both drivers would be tied down to long-boards made it highly doubtful that they would get into fisticuffs.

Roman sent the equipment over to Dexter with one of the firemen while he stayed with his Spanish-speaking patient. The firemen were more than willing to help immobilize and lift the large black man to the stretcher and then to the ambulance. Dexter had to use an extra- large rigid cervical collar on his patient, who just barely fit onto the 77 inch long, 36 inch wide, 1 inch thick long-board. The three straps that were designed to hold the patient to the long board barely fit around the man's chest and waist. Once inside the ambulance, the short fire lieutenant came onto the ambulance and got very close to the black man.

"Listen brother, here's a coupla sticks of gum. Chew this before you talk to the police, if you know what I mean..." whispered the short pencil-thin Italian into the burly man's ear. "If you want, I can have one of my men go with you to the hospital. I'll do it, I'll have someone go with you to the hospital."

"No, thanks" said the patient staring into the little man's face. "But I appreciate it, brother."

The little Italian white man and the big beefy black man then shook hands and held their grip for a long second. This show of togetherness and loyalty by two contrasting individuals from apparently totally different sides of the cultural tracks was just another piece of the baffling puzzle to Dexter, but it was interrupted by the knock of a police officer to the rear ambulance door.

As the little Italian fireman stepped from the ambulance, he looked at Dexter and said, "Hey buddy, please take care of him. He's a brother fireman from a Manhattan battalion."

"Of course. Don't worry, I'll look out for him," smiled Dexter, with the puzzle solved.

"Mr. Williams, here are your driver's license and registration. We weren't able to find your insurance ID in the glove compartment, but that's not a problem," said the officer from the door as he stepped up into the ambulance and handed the patient on the stretcher his documents, then stepped back down.

Roman called out to Dexter from the back door of the ambulance as the police officer stepped out. He had gotten a few of the firemen to assist him in bringing the boarded Mexican to the ambulance and was ready to put him into the ambulance.

"Hey, Primo," called out one of the neighborhood crack-heads as he approached the Mexican driver.

"He's okay, just do me a favor and stay over there out of the way," said Dexter.

"But thass my brudder, I want to help heem," said the grizzled man in the tattered clothes, with a thick Spanish accent.

"If this is your brother, help me out. What's his name?"

"We call him Chulo."

"That's all good, but I need to know his first and last name."

"I don't know his real name, just his street name," said the grizzly one, inching closer to the driver, extending one hand out trying to stroke the Mexican's forehead with feigned and over dramatic concern.

"Listen papa, you have to step back now. If you really know this guy at least give me his age or address," said Dexter, knowing that the crack-head didn't know. He knew that this was a ploy, trying to befriend this unwitting and dazed soul into entrusting his keys or cellphone to the crack-head, who would then turn around and sell it to the first person he could, for cash to buy more drugs.

Dexter sat in the captain's chair, near the front of the ambulance, facing toward the back door of the ambulance, beginning the paperwork on his two patients and wondering where was his partner. He had the Mexican on a long-board on the ambulance bench along the long wall and the off-duty fireman on a long-board on the stretcher that was bolted to the floor, both laying side by side approximately two feet apart. Both had their heads toward the front of the vehicle and their feet closer to the back.

Dexter took a quick peek out the opening between the rear patient's compartment and the front driver's cab to see if he could find Roman. He spotted Roman standing near the passenger side front bumper talking on his cell phone and apparently looking for the person he was talking to. A little pissed, Dexter began taking blood pressures and vital signs on his two patients, by himself, starting with Mr. Williams.

After getting two sets of vital signs and doing a quick physical exam on both patients, he also splinted the swollen and sore right wrist of the Mexican patient and finished getting their individual personal and medical information for the ambulance report. He glanced out the window again and saw Roman talking with a well-dressed young man who was writing notes from what Roman was saying. They shook hands and the well-dressed young man went over to the vehicles and starting taking pictures with a small camera. Roman walked over to the ambulance.

Cop or reporter wondered Dexter, who was fuming but did not let on. Roman opened the back door and sheepishly peeked in.

Sorry partner, I bumped into an old friend of mine and got carried away. We ready?" asked Roman.

"We've *been* ready. Waiting for you, rook," said Dexter steaming. He thought about making an issue of the incident later, but being that this would probably be the last call of the night, after cleaning, restocking and finishing up paperwork, and then he would be going on vacation for a week, he decided to let it go. Besides, knowing Roman, it was probably another one of his hustles and Dexter didn't want to know about it.

"Alright sir, we are finally headed to the hospital," said Dexter to Williams, and "Vamados a hospital," to the Mexican.

"You know what? I don't know which they fight harder for, making sure they get their people in, or making sure they keep us out. But once you get in, most of them consider you part of the family, even if it's as the bastard step-child," said Williams looking at Dexter. "Did you see the way the lieutenant and the little guy looked out for me? And I don't even know them. But you saw how some of the other redneck firefighters made little or no effort to help, right?"

"I remember when I first came to the department twelve years ago, one of the older firemen told me point blank 'there are two reasons why there weren't a lot of black firemen: they aren't smart enough to pass the entry test and they don't have the balls to go into burning buildings.' Can you believe that?"

Sometimes Dexter enjoyed the trip to the hospital immensely. The small-talk that occurred enroute to the hospital could be funny, lively, enlightening, informative or profound. Sometimes it was toxic, challenging or combative. Here, he was enjoying a black NYC firefighter airing the New York City Fire Department's dirty laundry and offering an insider's perspective.

"Our association of black firefighters, the Vulcans, filed a federal lawsuit against the City of New York and the

Fire Department of New York, requesting the federal government study the discriminatory hiring and promotional practices of the fire department," declared Williams. "The feds heard the preliminary case and agreed, making it a federal case. It got renamed, United States v. City of New York. Now, you *know* a case is serious when the 'feds' join in against a big city like New York and take your side," chuckled the black fireman.

      STILL PISSED ABOUT the Roman incident, Dexter walked slowly to his car in the SoBro Ambulance parking lot as his 11pm to 7am shift ended that Sunday morning. He kicked himself for not saying anything to Roman about it, but shrugged it off at the thought of going to his new girlfriend, Josette's, apartment for breakfast and R&R, rocking and rolling in bed.

She was a full breasted, big hipped light-skinned woman that was amazingly athletic. She kept herself toned and in shape by jogging a mile on her treadmill three days a week, roller skated every Tuesday night and taught an African dance class to young girls every Thursday night. Thirty years old and an assistant principle at a middle school for mentally handicapped children, she was a career minded woman who had a Masters' degree and her ducks in order. Dexter enjoyed having the doorman of her apartment complex open the lobby door for him as he entered the building. He took the elevator to eighth floor and was about to knock on the apartment door when it was unlocked and slowly opened.

      "Don't stand there shocked. The doorman always calls me on the intercom and lets me know whenever visitors arrive," said Josette. As Dexter entered the apartment she closed the door.

"I have to remember to slip him a bill one day so I can sneak up on you one time," he said as he put his arms around her waist and kissed her, noticing that she was dressed only in a thin black and white Japanese kimono, tied loosely at the waist. She returned his kiss with a ferocity that surprised him.

He knew from the passion of her kiss that breakfast was going to be put on hold. He was glad that he decided to shower and gargle before leaving the job. She was already pulling off his shirt and he was barely through the door, he thought, not a bad way to start a vacation.

They met through a mutual friend at a hospital charity event in the spring four months ago, but it started getting serious two months ago. Her job and other activities kept her busy and he was involved in a Paramedic training course at the community college, besides working full-time. Although they got along very well, their schedules conflicted and it took two months for the relationship to get off the ground.

He jokingly teased her and called her a cougar, prowling for young meat at the charity event. She would reply that she almost threw him back because he was too young and she didn't like dealing with young mentally challenged men *off the job*, too.

Dexter enjoyed being with her, she was almost always positive and quick to laugh without being goofy. He loved her infectious laugh and great sense of humor. She appeared to be the complete package, a wonderful product of the mean-streets of the South Bronx.

CHAPTER

2

RICO ENTERED THE OLD auto-body repair shop through the front customer's door. The noise from the machinery, conversations and radios seemed to be magnified as it bounced off the bare cinder-block walls. The ten workers sounded like twenty. He didn't remember it being this loud when he worked here years ago. He searched the sweaty grimy faces of the workers as they worked under, over and on the autos in their section of the garage. Not recognizing any of the faces, he turned and started to leave.

Outside the shop he leaned on one of the cars about ten feet from the door and began to smoke a cigarette. The mob had set up this garage and body shop as a front for one of their chop shops. Cars that were stolen or used in crimes were brought to this garage and disassembled, or chopped, with their vehicle identification numbers and serial numbers erased. The cars would then be sold for their individual parts, which would usually be worth more than twice the value of the car as a whole. Auto theft is an estimated 7.5

billion dollar business and continues to grow. Rico chuckled as he puffed on his cigarette. The auto insurance industry claims a car is stolen every sixty seconds, and that might make the general public believe the auto insurance industry is bordering on the brink of financial collapse, yet the auto insurance industry has reeled in record highs in profits over the past decade. Who is really the criminal in that picture, he thought.

The mob had wisely selected a moderately sized garage in the Hunts Point section of the Bronx, known for its junk yards, auto shops, factories and hookers. It was also known for the Hunts Point Market, one of the largest produce terminals and drop off locations on the east coast for tractor-trailers from all over the country, and all over the world, to deliver produce on a 24/7 basis. The result was a constant flow of large trucks and tractor-trailers through the community dropping off vast amounts of produce, and smaller retail trucks picking up produce for restaurants and stores, on a nearly twenty-four hour scale.

The chop shop blended in with its surroundings and was conveniently less than a mile east from Interstate 95 and the Bruckner Expressway. Manhattan was fifteen minutes away, and the trip to New Jersey or Connecticut was an easy thirty minutes from the garage on I-95.

The Hunts Point area was residential next to the highway, with five story apartment buildings crammed side by side into the first five blocks on the east side of the highway, traveling away from the highway. After that the garages, one city-block long factories and city-block long junk yards prevailed for a few miles ending up at the East River.

"Yo man, get off the car," came a voice from behind Rico.

He turned his head slightly and continued puffing his cigarette.

"Yo, didn't you hear what I said, man? Get the fuck off the car," said the tall Latino in the uniform of the ghetto – blue jeans, an oversized white tee shirt and an oversized baseball cap worn cocked to the side, off-center.

Rico continued smoking his cigarette and watched him approach, sizing up the young punk and noting where his body weaknesses were, just from his body type and walk. In a slow controlled manner, he blew out the little bit of smoke remaining in his lungs and said, "I don't know who you are but you better check yourself, homey."

"The only thing I 'better' do is wax that ass if you don't get the hell off my car," he said coming threateningly closer so that the two men were about five feet apart. Rico could observe that the young skinny punk was unarmed, but after a stint in prison he learned to not take any chances and make the first blow count. Young guys were always quick to cover their face, exposing their ribs, and skinny guys were easy marks for one punch fractured ribs to the lower floating ribs and the debilitating pain that it caused. Rico was ready, willing and able to rumble. He hadn't had a good throw down since he got out of jail. Rico took a small drag and blew out a ring of smoke. The skinny kid predictably tried to quick-sneak a right handed sucker punch to Rico's left jaw, but Rico saw it coming. He blocked it with his left arm and instinctively returned a right counter to the ribs that he put everything into. The young punk was momentarily paralyzed from the pain and Rico followed with a left hook to the jaw that sent the baseball cap flying and the punk sprawling backward.

"Rico. Rico," boomed a voice from the doorway of the garage.

Rico kept his stare on the dazed punk. Don't trust this guy and give him an opening 'cause he will surely take it, he thought.

"Awright, awright. Break it up. Hector, what the fuck are you trying to do, invite the cops inside? Get back to the garage and start workin'," said the voice to the punk from a few feet away. "And be grateful I saved your skinny little ass. My nephew eats lil wise-asses like you for snack. "

As the punk walked away, Rico and the voice embraced. The voice then grabbed Rico's shoulders and held him away at arms distance and looked him over. "You look good, kid. You filled out, like they were feedin' you raw meat in there. How long you been out?"

Rico nodded at the two muscle-men on either side of the voice. Both bodyguards were a size too big for their shirts and sports coats, with muscles screaming to burst out of their clothing jails. Both were eye-balling Rico and scanning anything and everything in sight for potential harm to their leader. Neither one nodded back or acknowledged Rico, but continued to stand a protective arms distance beside Sal.

"Been out a month and a half, Uncle Sal. You look well, and I like the Secret Service look of these two. The only thing missing is the earpiece and the government issued sunglasses," teased Rico.

"You got a place to stay?"

"Yeah, staying with my cousin in the Bronx. She hooked me up with a job at the law firm she works for."

"You know you can always come back here and work at the shop if things don't work out. I'd make you the supervisor here and have you running things. The boss put the shop in the Puerto Ricans name, after you and the crew got busted, just to keep the feds off our backs. But we run it and supply them with the cash and main business. I come around to make sure they don't fuck it up, and to collect the boss' cut."

"Thanks Uncle Sal, but I gotta lay low. Trying to go legit for a while and stay outta trouble."

"Yeah, I know. We all say that when we get outta the can, nobody wants to go back, but when reality checks in and we need quick cash, life makes us all hypocrites."
"Well, when I was locked up I started reading the law books to appeal my case and I got into it deep. I read a prisoners' self-help litigation guide and actually liked reading and studying the law, Uncle Sal. Next thing you know I got my sentence reduced, then I was helping guys appeal their cases and got a few guys out. I got a rep as a jailhouse lawyer and guys were throwing cigarettes, drugs, their sisters, everything at me to review and take their cases. The guards even gave me respect when I got a couple of them reductions in their child support."
"You was always a smart kid. How's your mom? You know I checked in on her every month, and the boss sent her some cash while you were away."
"Yeah, I know. She's fine and thanks you for stopping by with bread and stuff. She speaks highly of you and Tony G."
"It was the least I could do. Your father was like family to me. After he was shot I never forgot that we both vowed if either was killed, the one who lived would look after the other's 'familia'. Once you got pinched by the feds, no one was there to support and take care of your mom and sis, so I had to step up, with the help and approval of Tony G. And I

did it happily, 'cause I know your pop woulda done the same for me and my family."

"Look at you. You talking about them law books, but I heard from some birds that just got out. They were chirping about you boxing and kicking *molto* ass while in the joint. Just like your old man. He used to like to go to the gym and box the black and Puerto Rican boxers. And somehow, someway he kept that face smooth and handsome. Not because he was afraid to stick his face into the mix, but because not too many guys wanted to mix it up with him. He had grenades in both of his hands when he punched. He was a little bull.

"Must be in the blood Uncle Sal, 'cause I got the same love for boxing and I got the same grenades in both hands. And I don't think your boy from the shop woulda lasted much longer with the bombs I was exploding on him."

"Fuck him. I shoulda laid back and let you kick his ass a little bit more. He's a know-it-all wise-ass and thinks he's better than everyone else 'cause he can drive a tow-truck."

DEXTER DRIBBLED OVER half-court with his left hand in a fast-break, as his defender retreated five feet in front of him. Out of his peripheral vision he saw his wing man blurring down the right sidelines with his winded defender trying hopelessly to keep up. Dexter looked away for a second then threw a no-look, one bounce pass to the wingman who caught it in stride, then took one step and dunked the ball with aggression letting loose with a primal scream.

"Game," called Dexter. He walked off the court a winner for the fourth consecutive game. His basketball shorts and tank top were both saturated with perspiration. He sat down on the ground near the fence and pulled a bottle of water from his bag. It was half empty but still cool. Players from the opposing team filed by and slapped hands with him in a gesture of 'hood' sportsmanship. He had played enough for the day and let it be known to his teammates that he wasn't going to play anymore so that they should pick another player to take his place. He had a good workout running full court basketball this Saturday afternoon.

"Come on, playa. One more game. I'm about to school you, young boy, like you never been schooled before. Like I was your daddy. That's what you're gonna be callin' me after this game. Daddy!"

Dexter looked up from his seat on the ground and saw the 'little general'. A balding older gentleman who Dexter and his team beat two games ago. The 'little general' had assembled a team of veritable all-stars for this rematch and felt cheated that Dexter was leaving before he could exact his revenge. The little general looked to be about forty-five years old, five feet two inches and maybe one hundred ten pounds. Being six feet tall, one hundred and sixty-five pounds, Dexter posted him up close to the basket and scored with his patented back-board shot, every time the 'little general' guarded him on defense. This seemed to infuriate the 'little general', who was constantly barking instructions to his teammates on offense and defense, instructions that his team seemed to rarely acknowledge or follow.

"Sorry, Doc," smiled Dexter. "Gotta cut out. Got some things to do, but come back next week and I'll give you some personal tutoring. In the meantime, I can autograph your tee shirt or towel for you, no charge."

The little general smiled and extended his hand. "What's your name young blood? My name is Cliff."

"Dexter."

"You got a nice game, Dexter. You playing somewhere?"

"Nah, I played some D-3 ball at Lehman College for a couple of years. We won the City championship my last year there and I got MVP but I haven't played anywhere since then."

"Lehman College, here in the Bronx?"

"Yeah."

"Dexter, eh. You Jamaican?"

"Nah. My family is from North Carolina and New York. My old man was a serious jazz lover, especially horn players. He named me Dexter after Dexter Gordon, and my two brothers are Miles and Horace, after Miles Davis and Horace Silver."

Cliff was beckoned by the players to get on the court so that they could start the game. "Gotta go, it's Showtime," he said and trotted onto the court.

The first play of the game, the little general was dribbling the ball at the top of the key near the three point line barking instructions. "Yo, big man, post your player down low. White guy, keep cutting through the lane." Then he faked a pass to one of his players. When the defense overreacted and left him wide open, he got set and shot a two handed high arching set shot that seemed to touch clouds before it dropped through the basket. The little general looked over at Dexter and winked, then trotted down court, the male pattern bald spot on the top of his brown head glistened in the sun.

As Dexter walked back to his car, he threw his small game bag over his shoulder. He recognized that he still enjoyed playing basketball for many reasons. It enabled him to release pent up aggressions, get an enjoyable workout, and temporarily free his mind from any troubling stress in his life. It also amazed him how a few games of full court always seemed to help to relieve colds, headaches, sore throats and other minor symptoms. Today, except for a little post-balling exhaustion, he felt great. He probably could have played a few more games he thought, but he wanted to keep his usual routine going. Saturday afternoon typically meant a little ball, a little books and either dinner or a movie with Josette. He wanted to stay ahead of the reading in his paramedic class, so he stuck to a daily one hour reading session of the upcoming material before it was lectured. The course he was taking was through the State University of New York Community College and approved by the NYS Department of Health. His routine had served him well through the first half of the course and kept him in the top ten students academically.

The New York State Department of Health required individuals to take and pass both an eight hundred hour training course and a NYS 200 question paramedic exam, to receive certification to work as a paramedic in the state. Dexter had taken and passed the New York State Emergency Medical Technician course and currently worked as an EMT for South Bronx Ambulance, but he couldn't live on fourteen dollars an hour for the rest of his life. A paramedic job, although quadruple the training and commitment, would pay almost twice his current salary. His plan was to then get his bachelor's degree, and the rest of the academic requirements, then apply to medical school.

Basketball was his love, but basketball wasn't going to pay his rent or put new tires on his ride. He realized he had to put down the dream of playing in the NBA. Too much competition out there and, now with the influx of European players in the NBA, the competition was getting deeper.

He enjoyed and was very fascinated by medicine. Especially, the part of helping others, as corny as that sounds he often thought.   All of the countless hours of practicing jumpers, layups, free throws, dribbling drills and all the high school, summer league and college games were now replaced with hours of studying medicine and doing paramedic and hospital rotations.

The odds of a guy coming from his background, a black kid growing up in the Bronx, his father a truck driver and his mother a factory-worker, going to and graduating from medical school were slim, but he felt good about the outcome. He was determined and willing to put in the hard work and the time. However, first he had to pass this damn paramedic course.

RICO KNEW HE WAS A QUICK LEARNER and it became evident again at his new job working for a law firm. His cousin on his Puerto Rican mother's side had let him know about the opening. She helped him get an application and the subsequent interview. How he got the job was another story, either dumb luck on his part or sheer desperation on the law firm's part. He didn't hide the fact that he had a criminal record and expected that his application would be trashed immediately. He was surprised to get a call for an interview subsequently hired.

On his first day during training, the wife of Steven Spellman was orienting him on the policies and protocols of the law firm and telling him what his job responsibilities entailed as a new paralegal to the firm. He asked her, "Can you tell me in a nutshell what this law firm does?"

"This firm deals primarily with personal injury cases, or tort law, where someone has suffered injury to either their person or property, usually due to the fault or negligence of someone else. Do you have an understanding of tort law, Rico?" she asked.

Rico smiled at the elementary probing question, "Yes, I have an understanding of tort law and I am aware of the three elements of every tort action."

Mrs. Spellman smiled with arched eyebrows, but said nothing. Rico took that as another probing question and answered the unasked question, "The three elements are: Existence of a legal duty from the defendant to the plaintiff, breach of that duty, and damages suffered as a proximate result."

She probably felt, as an ex-con he only knew criminal law, Rico thought. But while in jail, he got a job working in the prison library that gave him access to any and all books in the prison collection. He read and absorbed every legal treatise and all the New York State Court cases he could find. He read cases from all three levels of the New York State Judicial System: the New York Supreme Court, the lower trial level court of the state; the New York Supreme Court Appellate Division, the intermediate court; and the New York Court of Appeals, the highest court in New York State.

"Impressive, Rico. You are a very intriguing individual," said Michelle Spellman, staring at Rico for a long moment. "Mr. Spellman wants the paralegals to obtain the necessary information, after filtering out the minutia and bs, to make it easy for him to determine if the firm has a winnable case against the other party.

"We get the facts of the occurrence, including information about the other party and their insurance coverage, then we send our clients to one of our doctors' offices to determine the severity of their physical injuries. If Mr. Spellman's doctors find a herniated disc in the client's back, but the client was only complaining of pain in the knee, we still sue the other party's insurance company for causing the client's medical condition."

"We have one client, Ms. Cruickshank, who we have represented in two auto accidents and one slip/fall injury. She gets a new car every couple of years from these lawsuits. Mind you, they are sub-compacts not luxury cars, but she works her pre-existing injuries to the max. The doctors keep her file active and any new injuries are exacerbations of her already proven older injuries. Mr. Spellman loves her and she loves Spellman, each smiles and hears a cash register ring when they see each other," she joked.

Rico watched Michelle Spellman as she talked. She was an attractive short Irish catholic woman. Her reddish-brown hair laid on her shoulders then hung down her back to her shoulder blades. He figured her to be in her mid-thirties and twenty years younger than Spellman. The evidence of many weekends on exotic beaches left her, like Spellman, with a beautifully bronzed complexion. She had piercing green eyes that were almost hypnotic to Rico and seemed to light up when she laughed.

He wondered what her background was as a youth. Did she grow up poor and marry the already established Spellman for security? Or was Spellman looking for a trophy wife and charmed the young, pretty intern out of her socks, and panties?

"So Spellman hustles the insurance companies for his clients and keeps one third of whatever he gets for them. He's happy, the doctors get paid so they are happy and the client gets a settlement and they are happy. I bet even the insurance company is happy," said Rico.

"Why do you think the insurance company is happy?"

"I'm a cynic. I think the game is rigged. The 'insurance game' is like the 'shell game' the con artists play on street corners. The insurance companies have the public watching accidents and car thefts stats, then they use those numbers to raise insurance rates. The public is so busy looking for the nut under the shell that they don't realize the nut isn't there. The insurance companies make money whether there is an accident or not, whether a car is stolen or not. If you don't have an accident for ten years do you get any of that money back? And don't you think the insurance company is investing your premiums into an interest bearing account somewhere? Something low risk like bonds or, if they are aggressive, certain types of stocks would be my guess. I like this situation that Spellman has going," said Rico.

"He prefers to maintain a certain order or decorum in the office and requires that the staff refer to him as "Mr." Spellman. He's a good man and helps a lot of people."

"Yes, he does. He has already helped me and I'm going to help him." Rico felt like he landed on a gold mine. He went to jail for ripping off cars and the greedy insurance industry, now just out of prison and he is back where he left off. He will be ripping off the greedy insurance industry again, but now he was doing it legally, from an attorney's office. He had already started scheming a plan to get a little slice of the pie for himself.

"I have some matters I have to take care of," said Mrs. Spellman, as she arose from the conference table that they were sitting at. "And, I am not as much of a stuck in the mud as Mr. Spellman, everyone here calls me Michelle. Wait here for Susan Berger, you need to sign a few papers."

"Please call me Michelle," she said placing her hand on top of Rico's on the table momentarily, then walked away.

Rico tried not to be so obvious but he watched her body move under the silky dress as she walked away. He could observe the panty line under her dress, the strong muscular development of her buttocks, and the exceptional development of her calf muscles as she walked. Probably a runner or a dancer, he thought.

CHAPTER

3

STEVEN SPELLMAN WAS A distinguished looking gentleman in his mid-fifties. Six foot-two, with a lean athletic build and a head full of thick silver almost collar length hair. Usually a tasteful and flamboyant dresser, today he was subdued with a dark gray five thousand dollar Italian suit, a white tailored and monogrammed shirt, a pale gray tie and kerchief ensemble with matching pale gray European shoes. When necessary he could be as charming, keen and witty as the best politicians, but usually he was an arrogant, sharp-tongued, mean-spirited individual, whose main purpose in life seemed to be to make more money than anybody else.

He arrived earlier than usual and parked his new black Jaguar XKE sedan in the back parking lot, but decided to walk around through the side alley of the building and make his entrance through the front. He was pleased to see the front of the building clean and the sidewalk swept, and further pleased to see the staff at the office on time. As he entered the main door he glanced at the wall and noted the green light on the security system above the numbers pad.

"Good morning, Mr. Spellman," said the receptionist as he entered the front door of the two story brick house that served as his law offices in the northeast section of the Bronx.

"Good morning, Carmen," returned the 'charming' Spellman.

As he walked through the waiting area to his office he called out to the receptionist,
"Carmen, is Rico in yet?"

"Yes Mr. Spellman, he's in his office interviewing a client."

"Good. When he is finished, please have him see me. Also, call my stockbroker, Tim and pass it on to my office on line one."

"Yes Mr. Spellman."

Spellman continued to his office, past the smaller offices on either side of the narrow hallway, cheerfully saying his 'good mornings' to the staff as he passed them. He had a settlement conference with one of the insurance companies scheduled for this afternoon and stood to settle one of his auto accident cases for nearly six figures, one third of which would be his customary fee. He was usually cheerful on settlement conference days and lately he seemed to have one scheduled every other day. His years of experience at negotiating with insurance companies had enabled him to learn all the tricks and nuances. He had become a master at squeezing every penny out of them and became adept at knowing when to befriend the insurance negotiator or intimidate and belittle them. He rarely went to trial with a case, but used trial as a threat knowing full well the insurance companies didn't want the legal expense of paying a law firm a half-million dollars to try a hundred thousand dollar case.

Another reason for the insurance companies' reluctance to go to trial was the fact that most of Spellman's cases occurred in the Bronx and would be tried in front of sympathetic Bronx juries that were 'pro' the plaintiff-little-man and hostile against large corporations. Bronx juries were well known for awarding ridiculously large sums of money to practically any injured party. But if an insurance company was persistent, he would hire a litigation specialist that relished going to trial, to handle his dirty work, and split the profits.

His law office consisted of himself and Michelle, his attorney wife, Howard, a recent law school graduate, Henry, an office manager/accountant, and a dozen paralegals or legal assistants, whom he liked to call his "LA's".

As Spellman turned the key and entered his office, it was almost as if he left the business-class section of an airplane and stepped into the first-class section. Where the reception area was furnished with frayed old chairs, worn carpet and faded wallpaper, his office was the model of contemporary office décor. Wall-to-wall plush gray carpet so thick that one's foot nearly sank an inch into it. A huge mahogany desk stood at the opposite end of the office facing the double entrance doors and all visitors. To the left of the desk was a large three- sectioned wall unit that had a stereo on the middle shelf, a few bottles of assorted wines, vodkas, brandies and cognacs, a thirty-two inch color television, and a modest sized legal library.

Like most professionals, Spellman had his ego wall that held his degrees, certificates, honors and recognition plaques behind his chair. And like many professionals he would explain that they were there for the clients and public's benefit.

Spellman had a good friend and law partner of fifteen years who died of a sudden massive heart attack ten years ago. His partner's son demanded half of the business and half of the profits, a percentage that Spellman was unwilling to give to a newly minted, unproven attorney. So Spellman sold his half of the law firm office to the son and used the money to put down on a better building in a better neighborhood.

Spellman then cultivated and nurtured his personal injury law firm into one of the best small law firms based in the Bronx. He ran his firm with a tight fist and an even tighter budget. He would annually donate his old computers and office equipment to the New York Public Schools system and they would return them saying the computers were hopelessly antiquated and couldn't be upgraded. Three quick knocks on the door caught Spellman's attention.

"It's open, come in."

Two men entered at the same time. The short balding man spoke first.

"Good morning, Steve."

"Good morning, Henry. I have a settlement conference with Allstate Insurance this afternoon, so I'll probably be gone for the afternoon unless you need me back here."

"Well, I do need you to sign a few things, but it can wait till tomorrow."

"No, Henry. I don't want to put anything off. Let's take care of the matter today, now."

"Okay, I'll go get the papers and come right back," and Henry turned and left the office leaving the other man standing in front of the closed doors facing Spellman.

"Rico, good morning."

"Good morning, Mr. Spellman."

"Have a seat. Let's talk."

Rico sat in one of the two plush high-backed brown leather chairs opposite Spellman's desk. He kept his file in his lap knowing that as usual he would be called on for the particulars within them at any minute.

At that moment a phone rang softly imitating a chirping bird.

"Yes, Carmen," said Spellman into an intercom.

"Mr. Spellman, I have your broker Tim on line one."

"Ah, yes. Thank you," said Spellman over the intercom. "Give me a moment," said Spellman to Rico as he picked up the phone.

"Hey Tim, how are you? Have you been working on that swing? You know I just hate taking your money." Pause.

"Listen Tim, I'm in the middle of something at the office, but I called to tell you to sell that business machines stock that I've had for a year. Yeah, the one that made about ten grand so far. Sell it all. I got a tip on another stock. I want to take the five grand outlay and the five grand profit and put it all on this new stock. I'll call you back later with the name but sell the business machines stock now."

Spellman hung up, wrote something down in his notes and then focused on Rico.

"Rico, sorry about that. Yesterday you were handling the new Gomez file. What is the liability?"

"Mr. Gomez was struck by a paper products delivery truck that was trying to beat the changing red light. Truck driver's company is insured by Patriot Insurance Company up to a two hundred thousand dollar maximum. Mr. Gomez suffered three cracked ribs and will require surgery for torn cartilage in his knee," said Rico, proud to have not needed to open the file for the info.

"How did we get this case?" asked Spellman.

"This case was referred to me through someone in my network," said Rico.

"Excellent. That was a good presentation. I have legal assistants whom it took a year before they could give as concise a synopsis of a case and the liability involved. But that brings me to say that I have been very impressed with you and the way you've ..."

The birds began chirping again. "Excuse me Mr. Spellman, but I have Dave your mechanic on line three."

"Okay, Carmen. I've got it."

"Hello, Dave. This is Steve Spellman. Did everything check out alright? Good. I'll be using the plane this weekend to fly down to Martha's Vineyard for a few days, so I'll need everything right. Thank you, Dave. How are you and the kids? Good. Listen Dave, I have to go. I have a client sitting in front of me in my office. Oh, one more thing, please put new tires on the wheels for me, okay? Good. Take care."

"I'm sorry, Rico. Where were we?" asked Spellman. "Ah, yes. I was saying that I have been impressed with your work ethic and your absorption of the legal tenets of personal injury law. You have a nose for this stuff son. Keep up the good work. I wanted to acknowledge that I've noticed your work and I'm watching you. I reward excellence, but I don't tolerate failure. Repeated failure is like a cancer and has to be eradicated...."

The bird begins chirping again. "Mr. Spellman, I have Mr. Griffith on line five from Nationwide Insurance."

"Fine, Carmen. Send it through," said Spellman as he picked up the phone while holding up one finger and giving the one-minute sign to Rico. "Mr. Griffith, how are you this bright, cheery morning? What can I do for you?"

"Seventy-five thousand? Mr. Griffith, your supervisor is a wise man. We are finally getting some movement and progress going here, however, I must say that my client was expecting something closer to our original settlement request of one hundred thousand dollars for his injuries. And if your company insists on this tactic of stalling and low balling, then I have no other choice but to proceed full ahead with our lawsuit in the Bronx Supreme Court."

"Yes, of course I will give my client notice of your offer, but I am certain that his response will be one of disappointment. Please reason with your supervisor and get back to me." Spellman said a polite goodbye and hung up.

At that moment there was a knock on the door.

"Come in," commanded Spellman.

"Steve, here are those papers I need signed," said Henry as he put them on Spellman's desk.

Rico sat there trying to remain cool, but he was annoyed and resentful over sitting in Spellman's office like a subservient, obedient little boy, while Spellman took care of his personal finances and expensive toys. This was a form of disrespect to Rico and the repressed prison mentality in him started to bubble up. Disrespect wasn't tolerated in prison, depending on the individual and the level of disrespect. The act of disrespect was like fighting words in prison and most forms of disrespect were met with violence and/or death. Rico started fidgeting with the file in his lap while sitting in the chair, fighting the urge to go over and deck Spellman then tell him that he better never disrespect him again. If he was fired, then it wasn't meant to be. But either way, a message would be sent about respect.

Was Spellman testing him and his temper, knowing he just got out of prison, wondered Rico.

"Okay, Henry. I will review them and sign them shortly. Give me a few minutes with Rico and I will get them back to you."

"Not a problem, Steve," and Henry left the office.

"Carmen, hold all my calls for the next fifteen minutes."

"Yes, Mr. Spellman," acknowledged Carmen over the intercom/phone system.

"Okay, Rico. As I was saying, I've been watching you. In each of the four paralegal, or LA offices, I have put one strong, experienced LA with a moderately experienced productive LA and a new LA. In your office you were the new LA, but you wound up blowing the strong, experienced LA out of the water in six months! I have watched, and been impressed by, your energy and ability to synthesize the personal injury game, break it down to its basic elemental parts, then make it work for you. By doing so, you have increased my revenues and in turn I am considering giving you an increase in responsibility and pay. I will give you my decision in a week or two. In the meantime, keep up the good work."

With that, Spellman stood up from his chair and extended a hand across the desk toward a surprised Rico. They shook and Rico left feeling a little taller. Mainly because he showed himself that he had self-discipline and self-control. He didn't fall for Spellman's little mind games, although kicking Spellman's ass ran across his mind. But Spellman is no fool, he probably has a revolver in his desk for any disgruntled clients, thought Rico.

INSIDE A CORNER of the Emergency Room at the Bronx Mercy Hospital, Roman was flirting with one of the female housekeeping staff while Dexter stood outside the triage room talking with a female member of the hospital security.

"I'm taking my daughter to Florida this weekend to visit a college there. She's being offered a basketball scholarship to go there, but I don't like the coach's philosophy. He pushes defense and wants to slow the offense down and run set offensive plays all the time," said the light-brown skinned, diminutive security officer.

"That could be considered a good thing. They say that defense wins championships," replied Dexter.

"Yeah, but my daughter's whole basketball life, she has played for coaches that have given her the reigns on offense and allowed her to run up-tempo, fast-break ball. That's what has made her one of the top rated point guards in girls' high school basketball on the east coast. She's a great decision maker and she can handle the rock," beamed the proud mom.

Dexter admired the passion that was coming from this little mom, both for her daughter and for the sport of basketball, the sport that captured his heart as a kid, The

City game. He wondered if the woman's daughter was as small as she was. Maybe five foot one. But the divorced mother had some nice wide flared out hips and wasn't that bad looking to have an eighteen year old, even with the drab unflattering hospital police uniform. Dexter hadn't figured out if she was being flirtatious, using the daily basketball banter, or whether she was just bragging, but she had become very knowledgeable of the sport and he enjoyed talking basketball with her during his visits to the ER while working his shifts.

She was the inner city version of the soccer mom from suburbia, he thought. Where the soccer mom from the suburbs transported their kids around in the family mini-van, many of the inner city moms walked or took subways and buses to and from practices and games. The suburbs soccer mom dropped the kids off, then came back and picked the kids up after everything was over. They rewarded their kid with praise to keep them working on building their social skills. Many of the inner city versions stayed and absorbed the nuances of the game and challenged, encouraged their kids to be better, the best. Their constant attention and involvement ensured that their child was treated fairly and not overlooked. The inner city version's intentions was also for the child to be involved in some social skills activity, getting some physical exercise, but there was a stronger urgency for the possibility of getting a scholarship to college through sports.

"SoBro unit for a 10-13 at South Bronx Hospital," called the dispatcher over Dexter's portable radio.

"Excuse me for a minute," said Dexter to the hospital security officer. "SoBro 1 at South Bronx Hospital, go ahead with your message."

"SoBro 1, I have received a 10-13 transmission from SoBro 3. Their last known location was having dropped off a patient at Bronx Mercy Hospital thirty minutes in the past," said the concerned dispatcher.

"SoBro 1, received. We'll assess and advise."

"Listen Denise, I gotta go," said Dexter while visually scanning the ER for Roman. Their eyes met and Roman nodded, then started walking toward Dexter near the entry/exit door to the ER.

Roman, or Romie, was a short muscular Caucasian Puerto Rican with a bronzed tan. He had smooth movie-star features, perfect teeth and medium length jet black hair. The dark blue EMS uniform muted his large shoulders, chest and back.

The dispatcher had called their unit to respond to a signal 10-13. It usually meant that one of the other ambulance units was either in route or on a scene involving a situation where they felt they were in danger of imminent harm to themselves or their patient, and needed assistance.

One of the two EMT's on SoBro 3, the unit calling for the 10-13, had a history of making inflammatory remarks which usually led to patients, and/or their family members, threateningly confronting the EMT.

"Is that Himmler and O'Neil on that crew tonight?"

"Yeah, but they're not around the ER," said Roman. "I think they left about fifteen minutes ago."

As they walked out to the ambulance bay, the only ambulance parked in the bay was theirs.

"Yo, you better get some more ambulance guys here to the Chicken Shack 'cause your boys are getting their ass' stomped," yelled an unidentified voice loudly over the radio.

Roman and Dexter exchanged quizzical looks at each other.

"Who the fuck was that?" asked Roman.

The dispatcher got on the air and asked the person speaking to identify and repeat their message several times, without response.

"You know what? I wonder if they're at Oscar's Rib and Chicken Shack over on 149th Street, ten blocks away," said Dexter.

They jumped in their ambulance and pulled out of the hospital bay lights and siren wailing. "Central, be advised, SoBro 3 is NOT at Bronx Mercy Hospital. SoBro 1 is headed over to 149 Street and Third Ave. We believe SoBro 3 is at that location," transmitted Dexter as he drove.

"Yes SoBro 1, we have received several calls from individuals who state that a fight is going on inside of the fast food restaurant at that location and that an ambulance crew may be involved."

"Central, do you have PD responding?" asked Roman.

"Yes, and an EMS Supervisor."

They arrived on the scene three minutes later to find three NYPD cars there and PD in control of the crowd inside of the Chicken Shack. The two EMT's were walking toward Roman and Dexter's ambulance, ripped shirts, bruised faces, bloodied lips and looking like hell.

"What the hell happened?" asked Roman.

"I dunno. I walked into the joint to get some chicken. A bunch of black guys were just standing and laughing for a few minutes, so I ordered. I thought they had ordered already. Next thing I know they were coming at me 'cause they felt I had jumped the line, so I picked up a chair and started swinging. Honest, that's what happened," said EMT Josef Himmler.

Dexter handed Himmler an ice pack for his face and a handful of bandages.

Later they heard another version of the story in the locker room at the end of the tour.

"Yo, man. Did you hear what your boy did this time?" asked SoBro EMT Andre Adams shaking his head.

"Yeah, we heard Himmler's version," chuckled Dexter.

"Listen to this shit," said Adams with his usual light stutter and animated tone, "that rat-bastard Himmler and O'Neil had taken a patient to Bronx Mercy Hospital and immediately snuck away to get something to eat, holding their signal without letting the dispatcher know that they were available for another call. The dispatcher believed them to be at the hospital. But Himmler and O'Neil were at the chicken joint where Himmler ordered before five black guys waiting in line. When they started yelling at him for jumping the line ahead of them, Himmler said "I work for EMS. Besides, what, you afraid I'm gonna get the last piece of chicken wings and watermelon?"

"One of the brothers said, "I don't give a shit who you work for. Who the fuck do you think you talking to? Do you know where you are?" Himmler must have realized that he had gone too far and that they were between him and the door. He threw a folding chair at the closest brother, then tried to jump behind the counter with the counter person and take refuge in the store office. But he was grabbed by one of the group, thrown on the floor and they stomped him. "

"Ain't that some shit, man? Damn Himmler can't even go into a chicken joint in the ghetto without opening his mouth and inciting a riot. A patron in the rib joint, picked up his radio off the floor and told the dispatcher that an EMS guy was getting his ass kicked and to send help, whereby O'Neil, who was asleep in the ambulance ran in to help Himmler. And even he got a dose of 'whup-ass' before the cops got there to break it up," said Adams grinning.

"You know what I think? I think he's on a one man crusade to get as many black and Puerto Rican guys arrested as he can, by inciting riots, then playing the victim. You know what I'm saying?" stated Adams.

"One day he's gonna push the wrong person's buttons. He's gonna piss off some bi-polar, manic depressive that didn't take his meds and he's gonna get stabbed in the neck with a butter knife," said Roman. "Maybe that'll teach his dumb ass."

RICO LEFT HIS DESK and took some papers from a file to the area of the firm where the supplies, fax machines and copiers were. He passed his cousin's office and stopped to say hello for a minute. After exchanging a few words with her, he walked to the copier. While making copies at the machine he became aware of Michelle Spellman on the other side of the room raising her voice angrily at one of the paralegals. Rico observed the fire and passion coming from the diminutive woman, liking what he saw. He didn't like passive, docile, submissive women. He was attracted to passionate, aggressive women, within limits. He began to see that maybe Spellman had misjudged her, thinking the love-struck young woman was a passive soul, but as time went by he began to see that what he thought was a little poodle was really an aggressive pit bull. Possibly the manipulative Spellman thought that he could mold and control her aggression, surmised Rico.

The paralegal tried to defend her actions to Michelle Spellman, but it only further enraged her and caused her to berate the woman's quality of work over the past month mercilessly. Although upset, the only thing raised was her voice. Her body language was poised as if she were merely making a point, without any flailing of the hands or threatening gestures. Once she made her point she walked away toward her office. Within a few minutes he became aware that she was back in the room again, but while gathering some forms she was sneaking peeks at him. He caught her watching him briefly then turning her eyes away when their eyes would meet. He quickly looked around the office to see if anyone else had noticed.

Rico smiled inwardly, flattered that she was interested and that he still had it, the pretty boy looks and the raw charm, but realized that this was a no-no. These were dangerous waters. He had to respect two unwritten rules. The first unwritten rule and accepted truth was that one didn't shit where one eats. Second, was that one didn't mess with a buddy's wife, and although Spellman wasn't his buddy, Rico anticipated that Spellman was gonna help him make a ton of money, so they were gonna be like buddies.

CHAPTER

4

WITH LIGHTS AND SIRENS ON, Roman weaved in and out of the few cars on the road, while responding to a call for an elderly woman experiencing 'Difficulty Breathing'. Many of the cars pulled over to allow him through, but a few kept on driving as if oblivious to the bright flashing lights in the darkness of the night and the blaring noise from the siren bouncing off the brick buildings.

Roman turned from Prospect Avenue, a wide two-lane street in either direction, onto a narrow side street. After traveling approximately one hundred feet, he heard "pop-pop."

"Did you hear that?" asked Dexter.

"Yeah, gun shots. Sounded like they were from down the block," said Roman, slowing down the ambulance.

"Should we let the dispatcher know to alert NYPD?"

"Nah, rook. You're over-reacting. You sure you're from the Bronx, man? You should be used to it by now, that shit goes on every night down here," said Roman as he stopped the ambulance and parked.

"And does that mean that you ain't gonna help this little old lady out, because you're scared of a few gun shots blocks away? C'mon Bronx boy, either strap 'em on, or grow a pair. Let's go," chided Roman.

"I got your Bronx boy, right here," snorted Dexter, grabbing his crotch with his free hand.

Dexter and Roman entered the five story apartment building through the main lobby and walked to the elevator, carrying the usual twenty-five pounds of equipment – stair chair, oxygen tank bag, automatic external defibrillator and EMT bag. Roman opened the door to the narrow elevator and they stepped in, as Dexter hit the number four on the control panel for the fourth floor. The door closed, but the elevator, lit only by a dim florescent light bulb, didn't move.

"Damn. You know, I'm sorry Dex, but I'm gonna put in a transfer. I love you bro, but I can't take too much more of these walk-ups. I'm gonna put in a request for a North Bronx unit or a Westchester unit, where the elevators work and don't smell like subway urinals in the middle of the summer."

"Romie, stop crying, you need to work off the rice and beans anyway. Besides, you're forgetting what you always say, 'the jungle is where the amazons live'."

"Yeah man, I'd go crazy with the flat-chested, flat-assed women in Westchester. But at least they got cars, jobs and apartments," chuckled Romie.

"Let me try the third or fifth floor buttons and see if they work," said Dexter as he pushed the third floor button, without a reaction, then the fifth floor button. A loud mechanical clang was heard and the elevator forcefully jerked upward.

As the elevator rose, both men read the usual juvenile literature penned on the walls in magic marker. One writing suggested that the reader call Nasty-Natasha, the whore, for good sex, and had a telephone number attached.

Another questioned the manhood of Fat Freddie, calling him a gay punk, while another writer proclaimed that he had sex with Jimmy's fat-assed mother and drew a picture of her sex organ. Finally, the elevator stopped at the fifth floor.

"Let's push the 4th floor button and see if it will take us down to the 4th floor," said Roman.

"C'mon Romie, I hate it when you play with the elevators. One day we're gonna get stuck in one of these suckers for hours because you won't walk up or down one flight of stairs.

Roman pressed the 4th floor button and the elevator jerked downward. Roman smiled at Dexter, but the smile was short-lived as the elevator continued past the 4th floor and stopped at the main floor.

Dexter shook his head and pressed the 5th floor button again. The elevator lurched upward. "Thanks for another sixty seconds of inhaling the delightful odor of elevator piss and allowing me to read more elevator comedy."

They got off at the fifth floor and walked one flight down to the fourth floor.
Dexter knocked on the apartment 4A door and loudly said, "Hello, this is EMS."

Someone inside mumbled something and unlocked the door. The door swung open and an elderly black woman standing behind the door waved them in. As they stepped in they observed little mounds of animal feces scattered near the apartment door. Next they observed small cats and kittens scampering about in the apartment. The odor from the cats, urine and feces was overpowering.

"Hello, Ma'am. My name is Dexter and my partner is Roman. What's your name?"

"Hello. My name is Judy."

"What's the problem tonight, Judy? Why did you call?" asked Dexter.

"I get very winded whenever I walk around, even if it's just to the bathroom, and I can't lay down flat in the bed at night. I have to sleep with three pillows under my head or else I can't breathe."

Dexter nodded and took out his stethoscope. He put the bell of the stethoscope to her back and listened to her lungs as she breathed in and out a few times. Just as he suspected, she was congested with fluid in her lungs. He looked down at her ankles and saw that they were swollen to twice the size of that for a small woman. He kneeled down and gently depressed the ankle area with his index finger for a second. She had the classic signs of acute pulmonary edema, or APE, which is usually a result of congestive heart failure, or CHF, although not all patients with pulmonary edema have heart disease. Pulmonary edema is one of the most common causes of hospital admissions in the United States.

As Dexter took a physical assessment and history from the patient and Roman got vital signs, Dexter was aware of the cats boldly walking between him and Judy, and through the space between his feet. He felt a few of the cats rub up against his ankles as he spoke to Judy, and gently tried to shoo them away. He made eye contact with Roman who discreetly made a head gesture toward the door, to which he nodded.

"Okay, Judy. We think you need to go to the hospital to get checked out for your shortness of breath. Why don't we grab your coat, pocketbook and keys, and head over to the Emergency Room. We're gonna put you in our wheelchair and give you some oxygen during the ride to help your breathing.

Judy nodded and pointed to a kitchen chair that had a coat and a pocketbook on it.

"How old are you again, Judy?" asked Dexter.

"How old do I look? I'm seventy-eight years old."

"Wow. You look great. I would have thought about sixty," lied Dexter as he and Roman applied oxygen to the patient and wheeled her out of the apartment, nimbly avoiding the toxic fields of cat feces that littered the floor like brown minefields.

Roman drove the ambulance from the scene, through the cover of night. Dexter took advantage of the lull and began to engage the patient in conversation as a calming mechanism. She had answered all of his questions in full sentences without showing any signs of shortness of breath while sitting still and her color was good, not bluish or with any evidence of cyanosis.

"How long have you lived in this building?"

"My goodness, I've lived here for about forty years, ever since my mother got ill. I moved in with her to take care of her and her cats when she was diagnosed with cancer."

"Then you've seen this neighborhood go through a dramatic transformation, haven't you?"

"Yes, indeed I have. It used to be a middle-class neighborhood. My mother was a teacher in the public school system. Our neighbors were postal workers, bus drivers and secretaries. Everyone was respectful and considerate, and they raised their children to be respectful and considerate too. That was the rule back then. Today, that's the exception. Very few in the neighborhood are respectful and considerate, and their children are worse. Drugs, crime, disease and graffiti everywhere. The young women dress like hoochies and are having their second baby by the time they are sixteen, and the young men use profanity every other word and are proudly in and out of jail like yearly vacations. It seems like they get so used to the over-sized prison clothes that when they get out, they buy over-sized regular clothes."

Dexter nodded; he understood. He lived for many years in the South Bronx. He knew that Judy's section of the Bronx was the poorest congressional districts in the nation and one of the largest racially segregated concentrations of poor people in the nation. The median household income of the area was approximately $8,000, where two thirds were Hispanic and one third black. One would expect those statistics from Alabama or Mississippi, not New York. Dexter was constantly awakened to this fact by virtue of his job as an EMT responding to 9-1-1 calls, where he was allowed into the homes of patients during their medical emergencies and witnessed the squalid conditions of the poorest of the poor, living in New York City Housing buildings.

"Why do you stay, Judy?"

"Where else am I gonna go? In this rent-controlled building I pay one hundred seventy five dollars a month for rent. I was trying to develop a career as a theatre dancer on Broadway when my mother got sick. I gave all that up to take care of her. I have no pension and I live off of social security and a little trust fund that pays peanuts.

"Judy, just out of curiosity, how many cats do you have?"

"Sixteen the last time I counted."

AS THEY LEFT THE EMERGENCY ROOM, Dexter remarked, "that last call was an easy call. The old lady was a sweetheart, maybe a hundred pounds soaking wet, and the elevator worked, for the most part, but those cats were driving me crazy. Between the smell and them constantly rubbing up against my leg, I had to get out of that apartment. It was creeping me out. Every time I looked up, there were three different cats standing there, staring at me."

"Yeah, man. I'm an animal lover, but the smell was buggin' me out. It was also messing with my asthma and allergies. The old broad had too many damned cats. There should be a health law. One or two cats should be the limit for small apartments and the elderly. Especially when they can't get around to clean up after their army of cats. But the good part is that she was probably the only one in the building that didn't have a mouse problem," chuckled Roman.

"Yeah, but do cats eat cockroaches too? You would think that she is someone's mother or grandmother, and that families would look out for their elderly. It's a shame that no one would call her or stop by occasionally to check up on her. Or even make arrangements to have others check up on her. Did I ever tell you about the call I had with the DOA and the cats?" asked Dexter.

"Nah. What happened?"

"We were called to the scene of a possible DOA. When we got there, NYPD had busted down the apartment door because neighbors hadn't seen the old lady for several days and a foul odor was coming from the apartment. We walked into that overpowering odor with NYPD to find cats walking all around the front of the apartment. Walking toward the bedroom, in the back of the apartment, we found two dead dogs on the floor near the bathroom. When we got to the bedroom we found the little old lady dead on the floor. Nothing unusual there, old folks die and no one knows until the odor of the dead body lights up the neighborhood, but the gruesome part of this call was that most of her face was gone, down to the skeletal bone," said Dexter shaking his head.

"What? What do you mean *gone*?" asked Roman in disbelief.

"Yeah, man. Gone. The dogs and cats got hungry after a few days of the not being fed because the old lady was dead. The dogs died from starvation. The cats' survival instinct kicked in and they ate the soft tissue off the old lady's face. Her cheeks, lips, nose, *gone*. I always wondered, what else would they have eaten if the body wasn't discovered for a few more days? Eyes, ears, breasts, genitalia?"

"Damn. That's some creepy shit, man. You think the cats would've eaten her snatch? " asked Roman.

"Man's best friend died with its master. The cats showed no allegiance to anyone except themselves. I'll never own a cat," said Dexter, shaking his head and then stopping ten feet from the front of their ambulance.

"What the hell…" as he walked closer, he strained his eyes and tilted his head, looking at the top corner of the ambulance. Roman stopped and walked over to the side of the ambulance where Dexter was standing and looked up at the corner of the ambulance. Three feet above the passenger's cab seat, in the front corner of the patient's compartment of the box of the ambulance, were two distinct entry holes the size of marbles.

"Bullet holes! I guess those shots last night were closer than we thought. Better let Bob know and have him contact PD. Damn, we're probably gonna have to do paperwork and write statements," grumbled Roman.

"Wait a minute. I almost get my head blown off and you're worried about paperwork?"

"Relax. Probably nobody was aiming at you. You know how these young dudes are, they watch too much tv! They shoot with the handle sideways and can't hit the side of a barn. Someone probably let loose a few rounds and it hit the ambulance."

"But you're missing the point. Whether they were aiming at me or not, I almost got my head blown off."

"Don't worry, little brother. I would've consoled big-legged Josette for you."

"HI. THIS WAY," said Rico as he walked the photographer and his assistant from the waiting room to Spellman's office. "Mr. Spellman is waiting for you in his office."

"Hello, Tommy. How are you? It's been a while," greeted Spellman as he arose from his chair.

"Yes, Steve, it's been a while. How have you been?"

"My stockbroker and my banker say all is well, so I guess all is well," chuckled Spellman. "You and I discussed this photo shoot last week. What I want to reiterate and make clear is that I want this to be a billboard size photo that's going to go on the elevated subway at Tremont Avenue and Westchester Avenue. I'm talking about a twenty-foot by thirty-foot billboard."

Rico stood in the doorway of Spellman's office and watched Spellman's exercise in ostentatious pomposity. He couldn't just put a picture of the scales of law or something synonymous with the law; he had to put a twenty by thirty billboard of himself up as an advertisement of his law firm.

Rico wondered if he was jealous of Spellman and whether he would do the same if it were his law firm? Besides, this was Spellman's money and his firm, if he felt that this was a wise business and marketing move then who was Rico to criticize.

"Yes, Tommy, I want to take a nice spread of pictures. Some with me standing in front of my law library, some with me sitting at my desk, some with me sitting and my wife standing next to me, and a few with my wife and I standing in front of my law library together. What do you think?" said Spellman.

"Sure. First, let's get the lighting set up and then take a few pictures to see how everything interacts and compliments each other. My assistant is going out to my car to get the rest of the lights, then we can see what we've got to work with."

"Listen Tommy, I'm paying you a lot of money. I don't want to hear any bullshit about 'let's see'. I want these pictures to come out fabulously. I want to get compliments and phone calls about how this billboard makes me look like a movie superstar. If necessary, call your make-up artist to come over here now, or call a film production company to come here with professional lighting systems to do this right. I don't care who you have to call, but you better call them now and this better get done right!"

"Take it easy, Steve. I know you are under a lot of pressure as a lawyer, but we've dealt on many occasions. You know the quality of my work and you should know that it's going to be done very professionally. I take great pride in my work and especially since you told me that Michelle is going to run for Judge, it will be of the highest quality."

Rico was mildly interested in the nugget of information that just fell from the photographer's lips. Since the hand touching incident, he avoided her, but caught her staring at him from her open office whenever he passed by. He knew that look and knew what she wanted. Although Steven Spellman looked fit, he had come to work late recently and the explained reason was that he was at a cardiologist for a checkup. Rico was aware that Spellman had enough money to buy truckloads of Viagra or a penis implant; but knew it's not quite the same thing. Rico knew that there were other factors that go into sex and love-making than just the body parts, and apparently Spellman wasn't supplying some of the other factors to his young wife.

CHAPTER

5

RICO SAT IN THE BIG CHAIR in Spellman's office as Spellman finished a conversation on the phone.

"I'm sorry Rico. Where were we? Ah, yes. I was saying that I have been impressed with your work ethic and your absorption of the legal tenets of personal injury law. You have a nose for this stuff, son. As of today I am offering you more responsibility and a substantial increase in salary. Is that something you might be interested in?" asked Spellman.

Rico was expecting it, but acted totally surprised. He was beginning to resent sitting in Spellman's office like a little obedient boy, while Spellman took care of his personal finances and expensive toy. He wasn't sure if Spellman was showing off, or like a Roman Emperor, just totally oblivious to an inconsequential pion, waiting there. "Mr. Spellman, thank you..." but before Rico could get out another syllable, the bird chirped.

"Mr. Spellman, there is a Mr. Stein on line five from Flowers Insurance Co. who wants to discuss a settlement offer."

"Carmen, please tell him I'm indisposed and will call him back. And Carmen, please hold my calls for fifteen minutes. Thank you."

"Okay Rico. I have made you an offer and asked if you were interested. Are you interested or do you need some time to consider the offer?"

"I'm sorry Mr. Spellman, but during all the interruptions and distractions it wasn't clear about any specifics with regard to how much of an increase in salary and what the changes were in my job description." Rico thought to himself, you don't bull-shit a bull-shitter. He wasn't going to jump on a little carrot like a blank promise of a salary increase without knowing HOW MUCH of a raise and WHAT was required. He was no rookie, and felt that he could play chess in Spellman's league.

"Ah yes, clarity and details," smiled Spellman. "You are right, Rico. I didn't touch upon any details, other than to say 'more responsibility and a substantial increase in salary'. I purposely left out the specifics to see your reaction, and you didn't disappoint me. You didn't jump on the bait, or the first smell of dollar signs. "

"In the six months that you have been with my firm you have nearly doubled the amount of cases that your office has brought to settlement, and/or in-court jury decisions. By doing so, you have increased my revenues and in turn, I am increasing your revenues, or should I say your salary. I am offering to double your base salary to $50,000 per year and add a bonus of one-half of 1% of every case that you bring into this office that either settles or wins a court decision. The .5% of one percent is based on the amount of legal fees received for this firm. The base salary is okay to publicize and will be paid in a weekly salary check, but the bonus agreement is confidential between you and me. No one must know about this agreement and that includes your wife, girlfriend, mother or anyone else. The bonus money will be paid monthly, off the books in cash," said Spellman.

"However, clarity is a beautiful thing and I want to make sure it is abundantly clear that you understand who runs the show here. With the money that I am about to begin paying you, if I say something needs to be done today at 7pm, then you drop all personal plans and make sure that the damned thing gets done at 7pm, without exception, without excuses and not at 7:01. I don't care if you're in bed with Beyonce or Jennifer Lopez. I don't tolerate failure well, and repeated failure, which is more than once, is like a cancer that must be eradicated. DO we understand each other?" asked Spellman in a forceful tone.

"Like you said, Mr. Spellman, clarity is a beautiful thing," smiled Rico.

"And keeping with the clarity theme, am I to understand that you accept my offer?" asked Spellman.

Rico had studied the cases that came into his LA office. The average case was a car accident with back injuries that the insurance companies would fight, stall and hardball about before settling for between fifty and 75,000 dollars. Spellman would get his one third, which would come to about fifteen to 25,000, and Rico would stand to get about 1,000 for each settled or awarded case. Quick math told him he could equal his new fifty thousand dollar annual salary with another fifty thousand in bonuses, for just a few extra hours of work.

Rico smiled, "Yes, Mr. Spellman, I accept your offer except for one small detail. I think a full one percent bonus would be more in order, considering the added cases I have helped bring into this office. Especially since you've indicated that I've helped double the amount of cases that my section has settled or won in court." Now, Rico felt, it was his turn to play chess and try to negotiate a better deal. He wanted to see how Spellman would handle a little pressure returned to him.

"I think I have made a very generous offer, Rico. However you must consider my situation. You are a diamond in the rough: above average IQ, charismatic, ruggedly handsome, very perceptive, with a high energy level and in great physical shape. But I have done a complete background check on you and I am aware of your criminal arrest and prison record. I have given you a fresh start with a new job, and now, a promotion. If things go well and you keep your nose clean I might be able to get you into the law school that I graduated from and currently sit on the board."

"You remind me a lot of myself; when I was a young man. I stayed in trouble for foolish, immature reasons. I was even in juvenile jail for a while and was exposed to both, the influence of the extreme criminal elements and the power of the law. Being confined to a community of murderers, sociopaths and psychopaths has an effect on a young mind. And seeing the power of the law, where it could just rip you from your home and cage you like an animal was eye-opening. Eventually I got my act together and started to realize that I was intelligent enough to make the law work for me. I studied business in college and kept a B+ average without really trying, then went to law school. My background wasn't detrimental because I was considered a youthful offender and my file was sealed," smiled Spellman.

"But enough of my reminiscing, if half of a percentage point is a deal breaker for you, then I can understand your feelings, and you can stay in your current position with this offer staying between the two of us. However, if you accept the offer as is, you might be able to request consideration for the half percentage raise down the road, depending on how you handle our current arrangement and your increased responsibilities.

"Mr. Spellman, I accept your generous offer and I am grateful for the opportunities you have given me and continue to give me." Rico had to humbly admit defeat. At first he felt that he had Spellman in a vulnerable bargaining position, having pulled in many accident cases for the firm, but Spellman pulled out the 'prison record' card. Rico gave Spellman the round. Check, not checkmate.

"A wise decision, son. First we have to work on your appearance. You will be going to court to file motions and papers for me, and represent my firm when speaking to clients and potential clients. You have to start dressing the part. You need to go to a men's clothing store and purchase a few pairs of dress slacks and sport coats combinations, along with some quality shirts and ties. Then I will send you over to my friend's auto dealership, so that you can purchase a good, reliable used car. Don't worry about your credit, he will extend you a line of credit to finance the car at my request, with affordable monthly payments that you'll be able to handle."

Rico took stock of his appearance in the reflection off Spellman's mirror in the wall unit beside him. He had considered his wardrobe cool and appropriate, compared to what the other paralegals wore. Rico's usual work uniform consisted of khakis with a golf shirt or buttoned down dress shirt. He usually wore loafers and based his attire on comfort, affordability and a GQ style of coolness. But, if Spellman wanted him to step up his appearance, and was going to increase his pay, then who was he to argue, he thought.

Spellman stood from behind his massive desk and extended his hand, the signal that Rico's audience with the emperor was over. Rico stood and shook Spellman's hand.

"I'll have Henry change your base salary right away. Also, I'll make the phone call to my friend at the dealership and get you the number to the contact person to make an appointment."

Rico was expecting some sort of carrot from Spellman for increasing the firm's caseload and income, and as a matter of fact, wondered why it took so long. He realized that Spellman was a tight-wad and he began to also realize that Spellman, underneath the glitz and polish, was a sleazy individual. Rico also believed that his arrangement with Spellman was a violation of the New York State Bar Association's Ethics Code and would put Spellman's license in jeopardy. It was clear Spellman didn't want to lose Rico, and wanted to continue a profitable arrangement with him, keeping all matters hush-hush.

As Rico left Spellman's office and walked back to his shared paralegal office, he began planning his strategy to increase the cases he attracted to the firm. He already had discreet arrangements with a few tow-truck guys he trusted from his past, a hospital admission clerk who was a relative, and a few ambulance workers he knew. They would contact him with info regarding serious accidents that resulted in injuries and he would do follow ups, discretely reaching out to the injured parties. If the injury resulted in a potential client and case, then Rico gave the informants an under-the-table fifty dollar finder's fee.

DEXTER HATED NURSING HOME CALLS, especially right before 7am, the end of the tour. The Nursing Home morning crew would do their rounds and check on each patient at the beginning of their shift. Occasionally they would find a patient who wasn't breathing. Following their protocols and procedures, they would initiate cardiopulmonary resuscitation (CPR) and dial 9-1-1. On a few of those occasions Dexter arrived to find the staff doing CPR on a patient that must have died after dinner, was presumed asleep for the night, and was literally stiff as a board with rigor mortis when the EMS crews arrived. When Dexter tried to turn or lift the head to check for a carotid pulse in the neck the whole body almost turned; it was so rigid. But today's call came in as a "Difficulty Breathing," in the Vent-Unit.

As Dexter and Roman entered the Nursing Home and headed toward the Vent-Unit, they were redirected toward another area. A NYPD officer, already on the scene, pointed toward a room with its door partially closed. Dexter and Roman stopped their rolling stretcher, loaded down with their equipment, and opened the door; they saw some of the Nursing Home staff performing CPR on a patient. Dexter and Roman entered the two-bed 10x15 foot room and the five person staff stepped aside, leaving a path for them to the patient. One little nurse at the side of the bed was doing compressions on the chest of a huge man, while another was holding an Ambu-bag over his face and squeezing it every fifteen seconds to supply oxygen to his lungs.

"Central be advised, have the medics expedite. Our Difficulty Breather is in Cardiac Arrest," said Dexter into his portable radio. At that moment a loud voice from the automatic external defibrillator declared, "Stop CPR, analyzing rhythm. Stop CPR, analyzing rhythm. NO shock indicated. No shock indicated. Resume CPR. Resume CPR."

Dexter gloved up and nodded to the tiny nurse doing CPR, then felt to determine there was indeed, no pulse. Dexter began visualizing the patient's chest to find his markings for the correct hand location for chest compressions when he fully realized the girth of the patient. His waist was as wide as the hospital bed. "Poor guy," he thought, then began CPR compressions on the patient's chest as Roman gloved up and took over ventilations on the patient.

"How long has the patient been down?" asked Dexter to no one in particular.

"The duty nurse found him with agonal breaths about 20 minutes ago, and CPR was begun immediately," replied an administrative looking woman clutching a clipboard to her chest.

"What is his medical history?" asked Dexter. At that moment a male and female paramedic crew entered the room. Dexter gave them the update. The salt and pepper haired male medic, Carl, stepped bedside the bed and took control. "Do we know if there is a DNR in effect?" he asked as he began attaching EKG electrodes to the patient. His eyes widened momentarily in mock shock at the patient's width. "Officer, can you clear the room and keep the door closed while we're working on the patient... we can try to give this gentleman a little privacy."

After the room cleared, Carl looked at Dexter and shook his head. "You can ease up on the CPR, this guy is gone. We're gonna go through the motions, give him a few rounds of drugs and call it," as he started an intravenous line in the patient's forearm.

"Hey Monica, how much does this guy weigh?" asked Roman, while doing ventilations.

"His chart says 378 lbs and that he is 58-years-old," said the female medic.

"Damn shame," said Roman. "He looks at least70. This guy is a perfect advertisement that fat kills." Dexter shook his head at Roman's usual bluntness and reminded himself to try to remind him of their talk on Roman's occasional appearance of insensitivity, as he continued CPR.

Carl called the Medical Control Doctor at Telemetry, presented the past and present history to the doctor and received approval to terminate treatment and pronounce the patient dead.

As the two crews gathered their equipment and bags, and placed a sheet over the dead patient's body, Roman and Carl's eyes met. Roman nodded, winked and said, "You're my hero, Carl. My back thanks you. This patient was a hernia waiting to happen and trying to lift him onto the ambulance stretcher was gonna make a hernia a reality."

JOSETTE WALKED THROUGH THE DOORS of the restaurant and was immediately greeted by the maître -d'. "Good evening, ma'am. How many in your party?"

"I am meeting a gentleman-friend for dinner. I believe he is here already," she smiled politely, while scanning the tables that were visible from the front waiting area.

"Ah, yes. You are the young lady that the gentleman is waiting for. Please follow me."

They approached the table; Dexter was reading a paramedic textbook and looked up. He stood, hugged her and they kissed lightly on the lips. He helped her take off a light jacket, pulled her chair out from the table and pushed it under her as she sat, watching her body as she eased into the chair.

"How was your day?" he asked, glancing around at the tables and patrons near them. Although he had heard the murmur of light chatter in the background and sounds of silverware on plates as people ate, he had been oblivious to those directly next to him as he studied his paramedic notes and books. The restaurant had a rich ethnic diversity, which he enjoyed. A casually dressed middle-aged Italian couple was closest to them, their voices barely audible.

"Fabulous. I thought about meeting you for dinner all day and it gave the day a special glow," replied Josette.

"I'm glad to hear that. We haven't been going out a lot lately, so I thought this would be nice change of flow," said Dexter. "As you know, I love seafood and this is one of the better seafood restaurants on City Island."

"I must say, baby, you look awesome. I love you in that pink dress. It exposes just the right amount of cleavage with that opening below the neck and it's kind of tight around your thick hips, which accentuates your thin waist."

"Be careful, Dex, you are treading on thin ice. I'm taking it as a compliment right now," warned Josette.

Dexter laughed at her sensitivity and mocked her menacing expression. "Just for the record, I love every millimeter of your hips and ass, but OK, I'll stop. Check out the menu -so we can order. I'm hungry. I didn't want to spoil my appetite so I waited for you, hoping that you wouldn't get stuck at work or get stuck in traffic."

She ordered light- a Caesar chicken salad with an iced peach tea. Dexter ordered the fried Admiral's Feast: flounder-shrimp-scallops-clams, with yellow rice and steamed vegetables. Although he really wanted a beer, he followed her lead and ordered an iced peach tea instead.

"How was your day?" she asked.

"My work day was good, although it ended with a DOA in a Nursing Home."

"I sometimes forget that you come into contact with some terrible things. Does that ever bother you?"

"Nah, after a while you get desensitized to it. The more horrific the call, it seems to desensitize you for the next one. I don't mean it to sound like I'm a robot, but this job toughens you up psychologically. But anyway, I don't want to bring work home. I have enough on my mind from work as it is," said Dexter, drinking his peach iced tea.

"What's bothering you, Dex? Is your job stressing you out? I asked you before, why don't you quit the job and just focus on school. You can move in with me until you graduate, I'll take care of you. I don't want to beg you and keep bringing it up, but we've discussed this."

"I love you, girl, and appreciate the offer, but it's not that serious. The job is okay, I still enjoy what I do and I like helping others. It's my partner that's becoming a bit of a problem."

"Your buddy, Roman? The guy you're always hanging out with? Sounds like you two need a separation or divorce," chuckled Josette.

"Like I said, it's not that serious."

"If you don't mind me asking, what is he doing that's a problem? And, how are you going to handle it?"

"Let's just say that his personal life is affecting his work obligations, which results in me picking up the slack. I wind up doing his work AND my work, which I didn't mind, at first. But it's continued for a while now and it's becoming annoying and frustrating."

"It's your call, baby, but it seems like you need to step to him and get in his ass," she said seriously.

"Yeah, I know. With anybody else, it's a no-brainer. But because it's *him*, it's not that easy. This is the guy who took me under his wing when I first got the job. He treated me like a little brother, took me to his house and fed me for the first few weeks until I got my first paycheck. His wife, Maria, sends food to work with him for me occasionally, even now, two years later. And his youngest of two sons, Ramon or Ray-Ray, who I've bonded with, has recently been diagnosed as autistic."

"Listen, baby. In my opinion, all of that is even more reason to step to him and address the situation. Talk to him now, before it gets out-of-hand and it gets ugly. If it's not corrected now, it could blow up down the road and you could really lose a good friend," declared Josette, as she sipped on her peach iced tea, then took a small spoon and gracefully removed one of the small slices of peach and ate it.

"Yeah, thanks for the input and advice. It's something I've got to think about and resolve soon," said Dexter as the waiter started putting their food on the table.

"If you treasure the friendship Dex, then 'sooner' is better."

"Yeah, I know. Can you pass me the ketchup and hot sauce?"

CHAPTER

6

DEXTER AND ROMAN LEFT THE EMERGENCY ROOM
after bringing an injured patient from an accident call,
Dexter stopped and peeked into the hospital's EMS crew
room, designated exclusively for on-duty ambulance crews,
and found it empty. Roman slowed his walk, following
Dexter's lead.

"Hey Romie, let's stop in here for a minute," said
Dexter, closing the door behind them. Dexter looked Roman
in the eyes and trying to mute his anger said, "Look Romie,
it is getting damn annoying with you disappearing to take
your Latin Love Doctor calls. You leave me alone and I wind
up taking the patients history, vital signs, give treatment,
and fill out reports, while you have phone sex with your love
of the week. You gotta tone it down, man. Tell your girls to

stop calling while you're at work or something. This shit is getting outta hand."

Roman started grinning. "You think I'm calling chicken-heads? Nah, Dex. Let's go outside, we can't talk in here." Roman led Dexter out of the crew room to some parked cars away from the hospital doors and near a curb. Dexter studied Roman's face as they stood under the dim light of a New York City street lamp while a few cars drove by them in the night with loud rap music blaring out of the open windows.

"Listen D, I got some extra cash comin' from an arrangement I got with this old buddy of mine who just started working at an attorney's office. This is off the books, on the down low type of stuff. "

"Romie, this sounds illegal. It sounds like some of that ambulance-chasing shit that some of those sleazy attorneys try. You could wind up in a cell with someone named Bubba wanting to make you his girlfriend."

"Nah, D. It's just between me and this guy. I call him from the scene of a serious motor vehicle accident, or trauma scene, and give him some info. He shows up and takes some quick pictures, maybe gets a few names of witnesses, then contacts the patients and offers to have his lawyer represent them with the chance that they get some serious money out of the deal. He gives me a fifty bucks 'finder's fee' for the phone call, and the other day he said that I would get another fifty bucks if it's a serious enough case, that it goes to court and wins money. Man, I've been making an extra hundred bucks a week. That's gravy money that's tax free and even sweeter because family court and the ex's can't touch it. "

"How long have you been doing this?"

"For a little over a month. But listen D, this is just between you and me. I ain't supposed to even tell Maria about this. If you want in, I can ask my boy to put you down or we can keep it between ourselves. We can split or alternate the finder's fee when we work together."

"Nah, Romie. Me and Bubba ain't gonna get along. You keep the money. I won't say anything to anybody." Dexter's anger had disappeared and was replaced by surprise and sadness. In the EMS field, one works with a partner usually for an eight or ten or twelve hour shift, anywhere from two to five days a week. It is easy to go from co-workers and acquaintances to good friends in a short period of time. Often when two individuals are confined to an ambulance for eight hours, sharing breakfast, lunch, dinner, coffee, bad pay, bad bosses, bad patients, and many life experiences, if the chemistry is right, they become like family.

"Romie, you and I have worked together for almost two years. Our chemistry works well, both professionally and personally. You've always invited me to your family barbecues and Yankee games with you and your sons. Your wife Maria and your two boys love me and treat me like a member of the family. Although there is a ten year age difference, you have treated me like a brother and I feel the same way about you. I respect your 15 years of experience as an EMT in New York City and in the beginning of the partnership I leaned on you for advice regarding patient care. After a couple of weeks, you started forcing me to handle the bulk of the medical duties, while you primarily handled the driving, equipment and vehicle duties. I chalked it up to burnout on your part and looked at it as having the benefit of strengthening my medical skills. I began to note the cynical nature and attitude that you frequently expressed regarding our calls and I tried to paint the calls with a more positive brush," said Dexter.

"You're scaring me, rookie. What the fuck are you doing, reading my eulogy? You sound like either I'm about to die from terminal cancer or you're about to turn me over to the cops. Which is it? What I'm doing ain't a big deal. Cut the melodrama, man."

"What I'm saying is, I love you like a brother and my advice to you, my brother, is to think long on what you're doing," said Dexter.

They had much in common, born and raised in the Bronx, but they had their disagreements. Dexter disagreed with Roman's chasing panties all over the city, especially since he envied Roman's family situation with a beautiful, wonderful wife and two sons.

Dexter was saddened that Romie was letting his marriage responsibilities and financial woes influence him to make a very bad decision. Romie felt that he was involved in a victimless crime, like johns or jaywalkers, and therefore was less likely to be prosecuted. He felt that no investigators would go out of their way for this type of crime when murders and drugs were so pervasive in the 'hood'. Dexter now understood the frequent momentary disappearances on ambulance calls, and Roman's recent urge to make cell-calls at awkward times. Dexter had attributed it to the Latin libido but it was rather the lack of pesos. Dexter had a bad premonition about Roman's decision.

His thoughts were brought back to reality, as the dispatcher called their unit to respond to a signal 10-13 over their portable radios. One of the other ambulance units was on the scene of a call and was transmitting that they were being attacked and needed assistance.

"Is that Himmler and O'Neil on that bus tonight?"

"Who else?" replied Dexter sarcastically.

"One day everyone should turn off their radios and not respond when they hear a 10-13 involving that asshole. He needs to get his ass kicked by some of the brothers in the hood, so that he keeps that KKK shit to himself. That little wise-ass fuck, Himmler, reminds me of a 'little Chihuahua', always barking ferociously but without the balls or meat to back it up" said Roman. "One of the rookies said they overheard him bragging to his partner in the locker room that he 'enjoyed being called a prick. It gave him a hard-on.' Can you imagine that? Nobody at the job can stand that guy and he loves it."

"Yeah, I believe it. In my psychology class they talked about guys like him. It usually goes back to their childhood. They are comfortable with resentment and seek it; because that's the environment they grew up in. One or both of the parents, or maybe the siblings, was critical and antagonistic. So, he got back at them by breaking or losing their prized possessions and when they called him a little prick he felt vindicated and powerful. Some kids enjoy being the class clown, some enjoy being the star jock, some are the lovers, but guys like Himmler enjoy getting attention by being the class prick. They feel a sense of power at controlling others reactions and they get a power hard-on from it."

Against his better judgment, Roman drove lights and sirens to the 10-13, although he didn't get as angry as usual when the drivers of the cars in front of them didn't honor the lights and sirens by pulling over to the right and stopping. As they pulled up to the scene, EMT Himmler was holding a bloodied bandage to his nose as he walked from the entrance of a five-story apartment building with his partner, EMT Sean O'Neil, following behind him. They cast a comical silhouette walking from the light of the streetlight into the shadows of the night, O'Neil at 6'3" and 300 pounds dwarfed Himmler at 5'3" and 160 pounds. Someone had cut out two cardboard characters from the movie 'Shrek' and put it up on the office bulletin board. Under the picture of the character Prince Farquad, they put Josef Himmler's name, and under the picture of the Prince's bodyguard/goon, they put Sean O'Neil's name. Dexter suspected Roman as the culprit, but he refused to take credit.

An NYPD officer that Dexter knew was walking out of the building that Himmler and O'Neil came out of. Dexter waved and beckoned for the officer to come over. "Hey, Soto. What did our guy do this time?"

"Your boy goes into an apartment in the ghetto and tells a pregnant black woman, who says that she can't walk, that he ain't gonna carry no two-hundred-pound jungle bunny, who is only two months pregnant, down no stairs. And besides, her feet ain't pregnant.' He says this in front of the boyfriend and the family. Luckily for your guy, the responding PD crew was coming up the stairs, otherwise he might have gotten more than punched in the nose by the pregnant woman," said the officer walking away and shaking his head in disbelief.

Dexter looked at Roman who was laughing so hard he was crying.

"SoBro One, are you cleared from that scene?" asked the dispatcher, "I have an active fire in progress."

"Yeah, SoBro One is clear from the scene," said Dexter grinning, trying to put his hand over the microphone and muffle Roman's roaring laughter next to him, while he transmitted an acknowledgement to the dispatcher.

Roman was still stifling laughter, as they pulled up to the fire scene, five minutes later. A few Fire Department trucks were parked in front of the scene with water hoses running from the hydrants into the building. The police presence had set up a perimeter around the front of the building denying entry to all and in effect setting up a stands for the few late night interested stragglers, mainly teens and young party goers.

While gathering their equipment, a Fire Department Lt. approached them. "Hi, EMS. We got an elderly woman in a first floor apartment that is wheel-chair bound and couldn't get out of the building. We've put out the fire and my men are doing their final checks. We need you guys to go into the woman's apartment to check her out. She'll need to be taken out of the apartment. My men will help you when you say the word."

"You said the fire is out? Is there any structural damage we should know about?" asked Roman.

"No, these New York City Housing buildings have cinderblock walls and don't catch fire easily. Some idiot set fire to a box-spring and mattress, then threw some recliner chairs and who knows what else on it, then added some sort of accelerant, probably gasoline. It burnt pretty hot, but luckily it started about 3 in the morning, so there weren't any kids or heavy pedestrian traffic in the hallway. It was easy to put out."

Dexter and Roman started rolling the wheel-chair with their equipment toward the building. Once inside, the

Lieutenant had a fireman lead them to the patient's apartment, which was at the furthest end of the hallway, away from the front entrance. Walking through the hallway, they had to walk through almost ankle high water and step over a few heavy hoses. The sounds of portable radios, voices and water sloshing was everywhere, from the movement of a dozen first responders on the scene. Roman quickly tired of lifting the loaded wheel-chair over the water hoses, and muttering under his breath, handed the oxygen bag and AED to Dexter, while he folded the wheel-chair. He carried the small trauma bag on one shoulder and the folded wheel-chair on his other shoulder.

Although the fire was out, thick smoke still hugged the eight foot high ceiling and hung down a few feet from it, for the length of the hallway. Dexter had to bend at the waist so he could see in front of him.

As they passed the heap of burnt smoldering furniture, the intense heat coming off the walls and mass, combined with the smoke and water, made Dexter appreciate what the fire guys have to go through. The smoldering heap had a scorched ring on the wall where the fire had burned. He was appreciative of the fact that this fire was out, yet the heat from it was still intense to him. What levels of heat do these guys experience during active, fully involved fires, he thought? And what about the junk they inhaled on a regular basis, which Dexter and Roman were inhaling now. He wondered how many firemen developed lung diseases later in life.

They were met at the apartment by another fireman, who led them to the elderly woman. She sat nervously in her own wheel-chair, breathing oxygen from an oxygen mask and tank provided by the fireman.

"Hello, ma'am," said Dex. "Are you having any pain or shortness of breath at this time?"

"No, I'm just shook up with all the noise and activity going on outside."

"Why do you have a wheel-chair?"

"I had a stroke a year ago and still have a little weakness and trouble with my left side."

"Well, we are going to take you to the hospital for a check-up, and to get you away from the smoke condition that's going on here, in the building and in your apartment," said Dexter, as Roman wheeled the ambulance wheel-chair next to her wheel-chair. "The smoke is coming in here under the door, and through the door every time we open it. You shouldn't stay here." He sensed apprehension from the woman.

"We can have PD call a family member and they can meet you at the hospital. After you get checked out, if everything is okay, you can go home with them for the night. Does that seem reasonable?" asked Dexter.

Roman smiled at the rookie's handling of the situation, allaying the woman's fears and worries. "Yes," he chimed in, "and if you're a good girl, maybe he'll get you a cup of coffee or tea, maybe even a shot of vodka."

The woman smiled and rolled her eyes at Roman, "you are bad."
"Yeah, I get that a lot."

They sat her in their wheel-chair and Roman wheeled her out of the apartment with a SoBro oxygen mask on her face, and an oxygen tank hanging from the back of the chair.

"You got your keys and purse, ma'am?" asked Dexter.

"Yes, thank you, son."

In the hall way, as they exited the apartment, the smoke and heat were still evident. A group of firemen came over to the woman and each grabbed an edge of the wheelchair. They lifted her a foot off the ground and began walking in unison toward the front exit, stepping over the water hoses effortlessly. "Mighty nice of them," thought Dexter.

AT THE END OF THE TOUR, Himmler and O'Neil's absence from the locker room was conspicuous. They were put Out Of Service after what became famously known as 'the Jungle Bunny Incident.' Himmler went to the ER to get seen and treated for his nose, which turned out to not be broken, and then to the precinct to file a report. Roman was telling the other crews about the police officer's version of the Himmler incident, the whole time with a wide smile on his face.

"Those two are bad news. I heard that they were NYPD before they came here. They resigned instead of being fired for harassing two gay guys kissing in a car. They made the gay guys strip down to their drawers on the scene to ensure there were no weapons or drugs, and stand there, handcuffed in public, as they searched the car. They both had EMT certification so they were able to get jobs right away with South Bronx Ambulance Company, and word is they are on FDNY's next hiring list."

"Do you ever notice that the little fuck, Himmler, never hangs out with the blacks or Puerto Ricans? O'Neill don't care, as long as there is beer and alcohol involved. But Himmler? Never."

"You know if it wasn't for Latinos, he would have never been hired by NYPD. In reality he should be kissing Puerto Rican ass whenever one passes by him," laughed Roman.

"What are you talking about?" asked George Koutros, the janitor and locker room loan-shark, changing clothes in the back of the locker room and waiting to collect on a loan from Andre Adams.

"The NYPD Hispanic society filed a federal discrimination lawsuit against NYPD back in the seventies. NYPD had a height requirement for hiring. I think the minimum was five feet nine inches tall. The Hispanic society argued that it was prejudiced against Hispanics who as a group were usually genetically shorter in height. They filed and won. It opened the flood gates for the hiring of short Hispanics, blacks, Asians, women and benefited short white guys like Himmler," said Roman.

Everyone in the small dank locker room got a chuckle out of Professor Roman's lecture on Race Relations History and the NYPD.

"That's amazing," exclaimed Dexter, "that black fireman we transported told me almost the same story a little while ago about the New York Fire Department. He said that the Black Firemen's Association, several years ago, filed a federal discrimination lawsuit against FDNY because of the 95% white male proportion in its ranks and they recently won. Now, FDNY is tripping all over itself to correct the situation as mandated by the federal courts. The power of the law and the courts is awesome."

"You know, now that I think about it, that's what Martin Luther King and the NAACP did to fight discrimination in the south back in the sixties. They started challenging all the Jim Crow laws as discriminatory, where blacks couldn't vote, go to good schools or eat in restaurants. Malcolm X and his people promoted the right to bear arms, shooting and killing in self-defense. They got their point across, but Martin Luther King and his people changed the landscape of the United States through the courts," remarked Dexter.

Roman and Dexter walked out of the locker room, signed out and walked toward their cars in the light of the early morning sun. Roman, in his jeans, NY Yanks leather bomber and tan Timberland boots, stopped by Dexter. "Yo, D. Remember our conversation. Please keep this between us, man. Give me your word it stays with us."

"Relax Romie, whose giving melodrama now? I give you my word. It stays between us. It hurts that you feel you even have to ask."

"Hey, D. I'm sorry, I just had to make sure. But, it's a beautiful morning. I'm gonna go home, get laid and sleep all day, then play with my boys. See you tonight." Roman got into his minivan with the limo tint windows, whose backseat cushions have seen more sex than the mattresses of the neighborhood motel, and pulled off.

As Roman drove home, Andre came walking with extra giddyup in his step from the sidewalk onto the parking lot toward the SoBro entrance, "Z'up, Dex?"

"Yo, GQ, I think George is in there waiting for you."

"Yeah, I know. I owe him some bread, but the g-g-greedy Greek fuck is gonna have to wait another week," stuttered Andre still walking briskly.

"You know what that means, right?" asked Dexter.

"Yeah, I know. He's gonna add more interest on the bread I owe and threaten to get one of his Greek, or

Russian, or whatever the fuck they are, boys on me. I can handle George. He's a p-p-pussy," waving his hand dismissively and then he walked into the building.

Dexter watched the figure disappear into the building. Andre had on a three-quarter length tan leather coat with sheepskin lining and trim around the collar, sleeves and bottom edges. A thick cream white scarf covered his neck and blended in with the white sheepskin lining around the collar. The designer jeans had razor sharp creases. On this day he was wearing a pair of tan Uggs ankle high boots that had a fleece lining inside that was exposed because Andre had folded them down about an inch.

What a shame, thought Dexter. Andre was a decent looking dude with smooth features, and a thin frame, that knew how to dress. He could easily have been a male model if he were interested in that field and have made a ton of money. But instead he blew his money on clothes, jewelry and drugs. He was deep in the hole to George for close to a grand, almost all of it due to drugs. The rumor on the job was that Andre had graduated from weed and was now heavily into crack/cocaine. He was able to avoid detection because SoBro Ambulance didn't have random drug testing beyond the initial hiring phase.

Dexter had used George on a few occasions, but they were only for a hundred dollars on each occasion and were repaid by the next payday. George usually didn't use the physical resource except as a last resort, and even then he would have Greek muscle just punch the tardy debtor around, taking care not to break anything or not cause enough of an injury that the debtor couldn't work the next day. It was simply a way of getting a message across and it almost always worked. Dexter was worried that Andre Adams would be the exception to the rule.

CHAPTER

7

RICO STOPPED AT THE RED LIGHT in his 'new' three-year-old BMW 325 sedan, patted the envelope stuffed with hundred dollar bills in his jacket and smiled. As the sun shone through the sunroof and warmed his face, he marveled at how far he had come in less than a year. From prison, to BMW's and fat paychecks, he just smiled. He was getting accustomed to these paydays now. This week's 'off the books' envelope, like the past several weeks, had been almost two thousand, not counting his regular paycheck which was now peanuts, and which he deposited directly into an account with a stockbroker firm, recommended by his uncle. His relationship with Spellman, although testy and sometimes annoying, was proving to be fruitful beyond his wildest dreams. Besides his salary, he watched and copied

Spellman's lead on stock market investments and was making almost double his 'on the books' salary in investments alone. He used some of that money to buy a two-bedroom condo in a pricey Westchester suburb, and to pay off the three-year-old fully loaded BMW he was driving around in. He was also looking into buying a three-family investment property in the Bronx near the Westchester border, that he planned to either put in his mother's name or use as a rental income and tax write-off.

He was now heading to spread some of the wealth and take care of a contact for leads that proved to be extremely lucrative. As he pulled into the nearly empty parking lot at the end of a large baseball field, he spotted the minivan at the other end of the lot. He eased the BMW over to the minivan.

The driver got out, smoking a cigarette, and walked around to the front passenger door. Rico popped the automatic locks open with one hand, while the other hand held the handle of a switchblade knife under his jacket. Rico always had a backup. The minivan driver opened the door and got into the BMW, sitting in the air-conditioned cab with luxurious leather and wood-grain paneling everywhere, and R&B music playing on the stereo.

"Hey Roman, what's up?" greeted Rico, extending his hand.

"My man, "the Don" Rico. You are like the Godfather, man," smiled Roman grabbing Rico's hand and embracing him.

Rico smiled and pressed three crisp new one hundred dollar bills into Roman's palm. "This is for you, Roman. One of your seeds turned into a nice fat tree for me.

And here is for the seed that you gave me this week. Keep it coming, bro."

"You know I will," smiled Roman. "If you need me for anything on the side, just call me."

"Thanks, I'll remember that. But listen, I gotta run, got some more business to take care of. Remember Roman, this is just between us." Roman nodded.

"I got a quick question for you, man."

"Go ahead, shoot."

"Sometimes we get these bullshit jobs, you know? Like where there's a car accident, but neither car has barely a scratch on it, and one of the drivers is sitting in the car writhing in pain complaining of head, neck and back pain to the point of, they can't walk," said Roman.

"Okay, I'm with you so far, keep going," replied Rico.

"In a scenario like that, should I call you or is that a waste of time?"

"It is very important that there be a serious injury. A lot of people are under the misconception that they can sue the insurance companies for any pain or injury whatsoever. But boo-boos and scrapes don't get it. Serious injury means a personal injury which results in death; dismemberment; significant disfigurement; a fracture; or an injury that prevents the injured person from performing their usual and customary daily activities for not less than ninety days," explained Rico. "I mean a boo-boo is a boo-boo, but if someone jams a finger in a car accident and they are a professional musician, like the guitarist I'm listening to now, then in that case the injury prevents him from performing his usual and customary livelihood. But the only way we can know if the injuries are serious is to get the client into our office and to our doctor. So, yes, do call me, even if the accident is minor and looks like BS. My boss is the kind of lawyer that will pat the client on the back with one hand while pushing them out the door with the other hand, once he has read a medical report without serious injuries."

"So if someone has a scrape, it's gonna be hard for them to get documentation from a doctor and hard to convince the insurance company that there is a serious injury worth receiving monetary compensation, but call me so we can get them into our office and get the details," continued Rico. "Like they say with the lotto …you never know…"

They embraced briefly. Roman left the car and headed back to his minivan. Rico eased away from Roman and the baseball field parking lot as his BMW purred. Rico contemplated his new found power as he drove and how the different sexes reacted to him and it. It seemed that the male contacts all wanted to befriend him and help him with other things, apparently for more money, while the female contacts wanted to sex him and spend more time with him, apparently for more money AND an attempt at controlling or manipulating him. He wasn't having either. Not that he didn't have occasional sex with a few of the female contacts, but he preferred to keep it strictly business.

Rico had done a three and a half year stint in prison for auto theft and belonging to an organized auto-theft ring. It wasn't his first, but he swore it would be his last. While in prison his good looks frequently got him into trouble. His intellect and his quick temper were the qualities that earned him respect among the rough and tough prison house leaders. Also, it didn't hurt that while in jail he took boxing lessons and was taken under the wing of an inmate who was an ex-New York State golden gloves champ. Because he was part Italian and had thunder in both hands he got the nickname 'Boom-Boom', after another famous Italian fighter. His hands helped him keep a few inmates off him because the number one commodity in prison is booty, more important than air or cigarettes. Some inmates would give up food for a week for some booty.

Rico remembered his first day, getting off the bus that delivered the new prisoners to prison. Some big black guy, six-feet-two and about two hundred fifty pounds walked over to Rico and menacingly growled, "Listen, you the new fish here. We could do this the easy way or the hard way, but your cute little white ass belongs to me. You will do whatever the fuck I tell you to do and you'll love it. You understand me, bitch?"

Rico dropped his personal items and in one quick motion threw a left-right combination that knocked the big black guy down. He wasn't ready for neither Rico's speed nor his power, and fell like a huge tree in the forest, but two of his buddies charged Rico. Before he knew it, the three had lifted him off the floor and slammed him to the ground, while he threw blows continuously. The three pummeled Rico as the rest of the inmates formed a circle around the fracas, blocking the guards view.

Rico was dazed and felt his pants being pulled down to his knees. His mind said get up and fight, but his body wouldn't, couldn't respond. Suddenly, everything stopped. The pack of wolves let him go and stepped back.

A large, brown hand was extended toward him. Still dazed, Rico reached for it twice before he grabbed it on the third try. When the hand pulled him up he stumbled forward. His pants were at his ankles! He pulled them up quickly. He noticed the blood on his fists, wasn't sure if it was his.

"Let's head to the medical office, Boom-Boom, you gotta get yourself checked out after falling down that flight of stairs" said the face and body connected to 'the hand'. "That was quite a show you put on back there," said the face. "You showed big balls and big heart. Even I woulda had a time with those three."

A prison guard suddenly materialized out of nowhere and tried to assist the staggering Rico, who shook him off. "Where were you when I was getting my ass kicked?" asked Rico.

"I got this Jake. The new guy fell down some stairs."

Rico's mind was clearing. He realized that it was being suggested that the worst thing he could do would be to point fingers and 'rat' on anyone. He would let this play out and handle it in time.

"I don't know what you did back there, but thanks, man. You probably literally saved my ass."

"Like I said, you didn't flinch once. You didn't back down. You showed tons of heart. That impressed me and my boys right away. The question was, whether it was a front, or was it real. You showed me it was real."

Rico stuck out his sore, swollen bloodied hand, "my name is Rico."

"Tank," said the rescuer, looking at Rico's hand. "Listen, you better get your hands taken care of. Your mind and your hands are your best friends in here.

That 'show' with the pack of wolves temporarily earned him respect and kept guys off him for a little while, until he started getting challenged by smaller, quicker inmates, then by groups. The name 'Boom-Boom' given to him by Tank stuck. He and Tank became good friends, and, as it turned out, Tank was the prison boxing champ and ex-New York State Golden Gloves Champ. Tank became his boxing mentor, coach and friend.

When not boxing, Rico spent a lot of time in the law library looking up law cases to get his case over-turned, or his jail time reduced. While in the law library he noticed how he soaked up the material like a sponge. The logic and rationale of jurisprudence was easy for him to grasp and he was easily able to memorize major laws, constitution, sentencing guidelines, and cases. He even remembered the dates, states, names of the parties and judges of any case he read. He helped a few inmates out of their cases and got credit for the partial dropping of charges and a few reductions in sentencing. The word spread like wildfire in the prison and he became respected and in high demand as the resident jailhouse lawyer.

Rico made his mixed ethnicity work for him while he was incarcerated. His Puerto Rican heritage enabled him to get along with the Latinos, and his Italian heritage helped him with the Italian and Arian groups.

"YO, D, I AM BEAT. I worked another overnight shift last night at the other ambulance company in Manhattan. It is starting to wear me out," moaned Roman, as he and Dexter drove the ambulance down East 138th Street, a busy, bustling and rough section of the South Bronx.

"So, why do all the overtime in the first place?" asked Dexter.

"You know why. Because that silly bitch is taking me on the 'family court merry-go-round'.

It seems like three quarters of my paycheck goes to her and family court. After taxes and family court, I'm taking home around three or four hundred dollars every two weeks. Who in the hell can live off that in New York City?" pleaded Roman.

East 138th Street in the Bronx was a cross between a major inner city thoroughfare and the marketplace of a third world country. Driving the approximate thirty blocks from one end to the other, one passed a police precinct, a fire station, a small supermarket, a bank, two or three bodega's on each block, several small Spanish-food restaurants, several liquor stores, several Chinese takeout restaurants, fruit stands out the back of car trunks, and a few Laundromats.

Also, there were the small businesses that catered to a specialty clientele in the community. They were the front stoop drug dealers and the sidewalk peddlers who sold everything from the latest black-market movies and music CD's to counterfeit designer clothes, jewelry and perfumes. There was also the heroin or crack addict trying to sell their most recently stolen wares, such as laptops, cell phones, and car stereos.

Even as they drove through the streets at the beginning of their tour, at eleven o'clock at night, every stop at a red light was an adventure. The last intersection adventure had a toothless, unshaven man in grimy jeans push a shopping cart full of boxes up to the ambulance while they stopped for a red light and asked Dexter if they wanted to buy power tools? Another younger man walked up behind the first and offered to sell a carton of Kool cigarettes for half price, taking a carton from a backpack filled with similar loose cartons with his dirty hands that were swollen, twice the size of their normal proportions: a consequence of years of abuse and shooting heroin into his veins.

At either end of 138th Street there were the obligatory public housing projects. Some of the buildings were as tall as fifteen stories high, with ten apartments on each floor. Like sardine cans, each tall building housed nearly five hundred low economic occupants.

As Roman drove eastbound he suddenly slowed down. Dexter looked at Roman's face to see why he slowed down. Dexter followed Roman's smile and fixed glare to two young Hispanic women standing in the brightly lit entry way of an apartment building, talking to each other. In their early twenties, they both had thick, firm bodies that they weren't trying to hide. They both had on cut-off jeans that were probably two sizes too small, cut high enough so that the bottom part of their tanned butts peaked out. Both also had on tight elastic tops that barely covered and held their breasts in place.

"Hey miss, can I talk to you for a minute?" yelled Roman from the driver's seat, over Dexter and out the side passenger window. The girl had seen the ambulance coming down the street and was watching. She smiled and waved. Roman smiled and beckoned her toward the ambulance. She walked over to the ambulance bringing her friend with her and stopped near the curb, "Hey mami, you standing over there looking all sweet like a lollypop, didn't I see you at the Latin Stars Club last weekend?"

The girl smiled in shock. "Yeah, I was there. I don't remember you. How do you remember me?"

"Cause you were the finest woman there and every time I wanted to talk to you, some dude was grabbing you to dance. I don't remember your friend, but she's fine too. My name is Roman and this is my friend Dexter…"

Just then the ambulance radio squawked, "SoBro 1 for an assignment."

Roman reached for the microphone and responded, "SoBro 1. Send it."

"SoBro 1, respond to a baby out the window at 999 East 135th Street in the backyard," calmly stated the EMS dispatcher over the radio.

"SoBro EMS received and enroute," replied Roman, while Dexter wrote the dispatch information on an ambulance call report.

"Listen mami, we got a call and I gotta go. Why don't you give me your number? I'll call you and we'll get together soon, okay?"

She smiled and told Roman her number. Roman winked at her and pulled off, putting on all of the emergency flashing lights and the siren.

"Damn, Dex. Did you see the body on that girl? I don't know what they feed these girls in the South Bronx, but she's gonna put a hurtin' on one of these young dudes with those hips. Ouch!"

"You haven't learned your lesson, have you?" asked Dexter.

"What are you talking about?" smiled a knowing Roman.

"Five minutes ago you were crying about your check going to family court and how tired you were from having to work a second job, then you turn around and get some chicken-head's telephone number."

"Taurus the bull, baby. And hung like a bull, too. I'm just me being me, Roman being Roman. I can't be anyone else."

"Anyway, this call is three blocks away. It sounds like it could be legit."

"C'mon Dex, you know this is bullshit. Most kids are in bed and asleep by ten o'clock. And besides, I'll hit chicken-head maybe once or twice, then move on. It ain't about love, it's about love making. "

"Get real, Romie. First, you know we see a lot of five-year-olds riding their tricycles on the sidewalk at one in the morning, while their mothers sit on the stoops drinking beer and smoking cigarettes. And second, all it takes is a broken condom and you got more baby-mama- drama. Again."

As they arrived at the location of the call, they found two NYPD sector cars on the scene already. Right or wrong, New York City has a policy where the police department dispatchers receive 9-1-1 calls first and dispatch it to their nearest available patrol cars. Then the call is routed to the FDNY-EMS dispatchers, who dispatch it to the nearest available ambulance. Sometimes NYPD arrives at the scene first; sometimes EMS arrives at the scene first. Dexter and Roman preferred that NYPD arrived to the scene before, or with them. It was reassuring to have two holstered weapons behind them in case the shit hit the fan. They have driven down the streets on many a hot summer night and heard the pop-pop-pop of gun fire a city block away.

They grabbed their equipment from the back of the ambulance and proceeded to walk quickly toward one of the officers waving frantically near an opening to the alleyway. As they approached, he pointed out the three steps descending down from the sidewalk level. They followed him through a narrow, three feet wide, twenty feet long, brick corridor that had about a dozen metal garbage cans lined up against one wall.   It was dimly lit with two forty-watt light bulbs dangling from the low ceiling at either end. As they approached the rear of the corridor it opened out to an outdoor alleyway between two adjacent apartment buildings. It looked like many of the occupants preferred to throw their garbage out the window, rather than fight with the mice and rats around the garbage cans.

The two buildings shared a thirty-foot wide by one hundred long common area of grass, discarded furniture, and tossed garbage. Standing near the middle of the dimly lit common area was two more NYPD officers with flashlights shining on an area in a grassy part of the alley. A third NYPD officer was shining his flashlight at a window high up near one of the top floors of the building.

As the two EMT's approached the two officers with the flashlights shining on the grassy area, Dexter could make out the form of a little girl face down in the grass and dirt. He dropped his equipment and quickly checked for a pulse. She had a weak pulse and he could see her chest rise and fall as she breathed. He touched her shoulder and called out to her seeking some sort of response. She cried out weakly for her mother.

"Do we know what happened?" asked Dexter to the officer with the flashlight.

"The mother of the child thought the kid was asleep. She left the kid on the bed in their fourth floor apartment and supposedly walked across the street to the bodega for cigarettes. She says she was only gone a few minutes. When she got back and checked on the kid, the kid was gone and the open window next to the bed had the window guard dangling by one screw. She looked out and saw the kid on the ground," said the officer.

As the officer gave the accounts, Dexter and Roman did an initial assessment of the patient, calmly but hurriedly immobilized the little girl's neck, then put her on a six-foot-long immobilization board to stabilize her spine with the help of the other officer, taking great care to be gentle and not to jostle her. After they turned her over and put her on the long board, Dexter began doing a physical exam, and the little girl began crying for her mother again.

A male and female officer had the sobbing mother off to the side, within viewing distance of the girl. Amazingly to Dexter, there were no open broken bones nor large amounts of blood all over the place, as one might expect from a fourth floor fall, and it made him suspicious of the story. However, there was bleeding from her mouth and nose. Her vital signs were stable and she had good, equal lung sounds on side only. The other lung sounds were diminished. He knew that no open fractures and no pools of blood, didn't mean that the girl wasn't hemorrhaging internally. And he was pretty certain that she had suffered at least a concussion type brain injury.

They gently lifted the patient on the long flat board off the ground. With one officer in front of them clearing the way and another behind them carrying their extra equipment, Dexter at the head and Roman at the feet walked, carrying the patient toward the alleyway. They lifted the patient a little higher, to avoid the garbage cans, and walked through the narrow alley. Once they had her loaded in the ambulance, the police sergeant said his officers would give them an escort to the hospital and bring the mother.

Roman called the dispatcher to have the emergency room on standby then put the lights and siren on. He followed the police car's lights and siren, sounding his own. NYPD had organized roadblocks at vital intersections along a route to the hospital, shutting down traffic at the intersections, until the escorted ambulance had driven passed. They arrived at the hospital within minutes of leaving the scene to find part of the emergency room staff waiting outside in anticipation and readiness, with a hospital stretcher ready to take the little girl into the ER, and upstairs to the Operating Room, if necessary. Their faces, all in deep focus on the little patient on the stretcher.

Something about trauma to babies and infants struck an empathetic chord in most people, and it was evident on this call, thought Dexter. Something about seeing little children bloodied and injured evoked feelings of sorrow, sympathy and the urge to protect them. Even cynical Roman, with fifteen years of EMS experience, seemed overly sensitive and concerned about the little girl's care. Maybe it was that many see 'their' child in the face of the injured child, but Dexter didn't have any children and he felt a paternal sense of compassion, sympathy and the urge to protect his young patient, as she moaned in pain and called out for her mother.

"HELLO RICO, IT'S ROMAN. Listen man, I'm sorry for calling you so late, but I was on a call you need to know about."

"Hey Roman. No problem, if you think it's important then I want you to call me. Talk to me, whazup?"

"We just brought this little girl to the hospital who fell out a fourth floor window. The kid suffered a concussion, fractured ribs, broken arm and a lacerated liver. She is in critical condition, but expected to live. Her name is Angel."

"Good call, Roman. I'm very glad you called me and you remembered to call me on the disposable cell phone. I don't care that it's two in the morning. It's sad what happened to the little girl, but this could be a huge case. I'm talking mega bucks. That little girl and her mother will be set for life. Hopefully she survives and goes on to live a healthy life. But I gotta move on it now, so we can have the opportunity to represent her and her family. Do you have her information for me?"

"Yeah." Just then, Dexter tapped Roman on the shoulder and made the coffee sign, a fist with the thumb and pinky extended outward, followed by the slight tilting of the fist up and down.

Rico nodded.

AS THEY WALKED OUT of the all-night coffee shop with their coffees and sandwiches, the radio squawked, "SoBro Ambulance One, respond to an unresponsive patient at the Grand Concourse and East 163rd Street."

"SoBro Ambulance received and enroute," responded Dexter calmly over his portable radio.

Roman was pissed, "What the hell, can't even get a break for a damn cup of coffee. I betcha Sanitation gets lunch breaks and coffee breaks. They haul trash, get twice the salary, and don't have to eat reheated coffee or soggy sandwiches. I'm in the wrong profession."

They responded with lights and sirens to the unresponsive call, with the untouched coffee and sandwiches on the middle console between the driver and passenger. They grabbed the appropriate equipment and entered the lobby of the apartment building. A short, thin, young, black man beckoned them toward the first floor apartment.

As they entered the apartment, a short, thin, older gentleman was laying on the floor with a woman crying inconsolably while she cradled his head gently in her lap.

Dexter got on his knees and checked for a pulse. He looked at Roman and shook his head.

"Please miss, move back and let us work on him. What happened?" asked Dexter, as he and Roman made space on the cramped living room floor and began CPR while connecting the patient to the automated external defibrillator.

While the family explained that the patient just got home from a card game at a neighbor's apartment upstairs, he complained of chest pain, then collapsed, Dexter realized that he knew this man on the floor! He looked closer at the lifeless features, he recognized him as Cliff, the 'Little General', from the basketball courts behind Yankee Stadium. He was amazed to hear the family say that he was sixty-five years old, without any major medical problems. The part about 'without major medical problems' wasn't amazing; it was him being 'sixty-five years old.'

He had seen the 'Little General' run up and down the courts like a twenty year old on many Saturday afternoons, shooting his patented high arching set-shot and barking directions at his younger teammates. Dexter admired his spunk and competitiveness, although it did get annoying at times. Now, to be doing CPR on him was surreal.

Dexter continued CPR with Roman and radioed for backup. He looked up at the faces of the family members and saw their disbelief and horror. He saw the resemblance of the young man that met them in the lobby to the Little General, and realized that he was probably the son. The pictures on the wall told the story of a good family man. A wedding picture showed a very young Little General and a very young wife. Another picture of the Little General in a U.S. Army sergeant's uniform and several family portraits with four children lined the wall in matching decorative frames.

Dexter heard the repeated bark, then whine, of a large dog from behind the closed door of the adjacent room. There on the wall next to the family pictures was a framed 8"x11" picture of a full-grown German shepherd. On the collar of the dog was a nameplate, inscribed "Sarge." How appropriate, thought Dexter, just keep him locked in that room. He doesn't need to get out and see me pumping on his master's chest.

The medics arrived and Dexter was relieved that they quickly decided to work the patient up and transport to the hospital, probably due to the fact of the patient's age, health, and that it was a witnessed arrest.

Dexter was further relieved that they got a return of pulses and vital signs while in the back of the ambulance en route to the hospital. At the hospital, the Little General was rushed upstairs to the ICU/CCU and monitored constantly around the clock. After identifying himself, Dexter checked in with the nurses a few times that night to get updates on the Little General's status and was relieved to hear that there was progress in his response to treatment.

CHAPTER

8

"HEY DEXTER, COME INTO THE OFFICE for a minute," called out Supervisor Robert Brogan, as Dexter walked by the office on his way to change into his uniform in the locker room.

"Whazup, Bob?"

Brogan nodded in the direction of a tall gawky looking blonde kid, about six-foot-two and all of about 120 pounds, maybe. Dexter observed that he was wearing a brand new South Bronx Ambulance uniform with razor sharp creases and marine-style spit shined black shoes. Dexter smiled at the utility belt that the new guy was wearing; it screamed 'overkill' and 'rookie'. Bandage scissors, eighteen inch Maglite, portable radio, pulse oximeter, carbon monoxide detector, stethoscope pouch with a top of the line three hundred dollar stethoscope, and a small 11-in-1 Leatherman tool were all shiny and visible in their individual compartments. It had everything on it but a coffee-maker, he thought.

Standing next to the gawky kid was a short woman who looked even shorter standing next to the skinny, six-foot-two human straw. She was rather plain looking, and, unlike most women who would have had on extra make-up or lipstick in an attempt to make a lasting first impression, everything about her was understated. Her hair was pulled back in a ponytail, exposing smooth white makeup-less skin and a fairly attractive face. She appeared to be about thirty-years-old with an untoned body.

"Dexter, these are our two new hires, David Newlin Jr. and Sandra Berry. They are both EMTs and will be riding for a few weeks with the night crews for orientation. David this is Dexter Reed. For one week you are gonna ride as a third person on the ambulance with Dexter --and Roman, the guy you met a few minutes ago. Dexter is a NYC celebrity that has been working here for a few years and is one of our best EMT's. He works the midnight shift and is going to paramedic school during the day." He then took a newspaper off his desk and handed it to Dexter. "Here movie star. Have you seen this yet?"

Newlin stuck out his hand and extended it to Dexter. "Glad to meet you. I've heard a lot of good things about you. I read the main story in the newspaper on how you and your partner saved the little girl; it was amazing."

"Thanks, good to meet you too," politely smiled Dexter, "but you can't believe everything you read or hear. I've been hearing about a raise for a year and haven't seen it yet. And if I'm one of their *"best EMT's"* and I'm getting the company, positive front-page press, then I definitely should have gotten one by now."

"You've been hanging around with Roman too long. You're starting to sound just like him," chided Supervisor Brogan. "Next, women by the dozens will be calling and stopping by everyday looking for you. Right?"

"Maybe I've been giving the women Roman's name instead of mine. Maybe those women have really been looking for me," said Dexter, upset at Brogan's disclosure of Roman's private business to strangers.

"Listen Dex, we can discuss raises at your next annual evaluation," he then turned to the female new hire. "This is Miss Sandra Berry, she will ride with you and Roman next week. For now, she's gonna ride with Himmler and O'Neil. Sandra this is Dexter Reed."

Sandra Berry stayed where she was standing, five-feet away from Dexter, gave a polite smile and nod in Dexter's direction. Dexter nodded back, noting her indifference. No need to rush to get to know her; the way this company and the EMS community worked, there would be a dossier on her spread verbally around the job within 72 hours, he thought.

"Say Dave, can you familiarize yourself with, and start checking, our ambulance? Roman and I will be out in a minute," said Dexter, as he left the office with the newspaper in his hand and headed to the locker rooms.

In the small, cramped, dimly lit South Bronx Ambulance locker rooms, in the back of the ambulance garage, Dexter changed from his street clothes to the summer uniform that the company gave - dark blue cargo style trousers with a dark blue short-sleeve button up shirt. The left shoulder of the shirt had the South Bronx Ambulance logo sewn on it, and the right shoulder had the New York State Emergency Medical Technician patch sewn on it.

"Silly Bob is already putting people's business on the street in front of the newjacks. He's spilling his guts to the newjacks about you, a married man and your women, and me, a dreaming nobody, going to medic school during the day," said Dexter to Roman dressing in the locker next to him.

"You know Bob is gonna try to feel the kid out and recruit him into the redneck gang with him and Himmler. But did you get a look at the beak on that kid? He looks like a cartoon character. Like Big Bird," laughed Roman. "What about the woman? Did she say anything to you?"

"Not at all. Why?"

"During introductions, I went to shake her hand hello, and she told me 'keep it in your pants, Reyes.' She's strange," said Roman wide-eyed and shaking his head in amazement.

"Brogan probably warned her about you, Roman the Romeo, and told her to be leery of you. Or maybe your reputation has reached other boroughs and other states," teased Dexter.

"Yeah, probably. Anyway, let's see what the kid's got. If he's okay, let him do all the work tonight and we just sit back. I could go for a night of doing nothing," sighed Roman.

"Romie, it seems like you have 'a night of doing nothing' *every night*. Hey, did you see the newspaper yet?"

"Yeah, I meant to call you. I've been getting phone calls all day about it. My wife bought ten newspapers just because our faces were on the front page with the little girl."

Dexter started reading the NYC newspaper article. Yes, Bob was right. Hell yeah, he was a celebrity. On the front page of one of the New York newspapers in large bold capital letters read "TOT CHEATS DEATH," with a blown up picture of Roman and Dexter treating the little crying girl with bandages, splints and oxygen mask while immobilized on a long board. He noted that the reporter referred to them as paramedics, not EMTs, and not by name. At least they didn't call them firemen, like they usually do.

"How did the newspaper get a photographer to the scene in the South Bronx so fast?"

"Probably some neighborhood freelance photographer listening to a NYPD scanner. Or maybe someone with a good cell phone camera sold the picture to the newspaper. We weren't on the scene for more than ten minutes," reasoned Roman.

AS ROMAN AND DEXTER DROVE to the donut shop around the corner on the way to their patrol/response area, they quizzed Dave Newlin. A soft rain was falling under the cover of night. They found out that he was twenty-five years old, two years older than Dexter, although he looked like an acned eighteen-year-old. An EMT for three years, he had a bachelor's degree and lived at home in Long Island with his father, who owned a mechanics shop, and his mom, a music teacher. Newlin served as an EMT primarily with his neighborhood volunteer ambulance corps on Long Island and although he was proud of his experience with the volunteer ambulance corps, Roman dismissed it as Boy Scouts work and not real 9-1-1 experience. Calls for cats stuck up trees and kids off their tricycles with little scrapes and boo-boos, while hysterical moms were having an anxiety attack, didn't count as legitimate 9-1-1 calls to Roman. Those were calls for the Uncle Johnny-type, usually the levelheaded male of the family or the neighborhood, who would arrive, assesses the situation, and calm everyone down. If necessary, an Uncle Johnny-type would take control and drive the sick or injured person to the emergency room himself in his own car.

"SoBro1 Ambulance, respond to East 141 Street for the OBS," squawked the dispatcher over the ambulance radio.

"SoBro1, send it," answered Dexter over the ambulance radio.

The dispatcher acknowledged and sent the call information to their ambulance computer terminal, a device installed into their dashboard and console. The information arrived seconds later on their built in computer screen.

"SoBro1 received and enroute," transmitted Dexter.

Roman turned and grinned at Newlin sitting in the back of the ambulance. "Have you ever delivered any babies before?"

"Nah, not yet."

"Well, then, the next question is: are you a virgin? Cause if you haven't had no pussy yet, you're gonna get the Vagina 101 class, while you're riding here in the Bronx," howled Roman loudly as he put on the emergency lights and siren.

Dexter took note of the differences of the three body languages as they proceeded to the call. The differences manifested the three different levels of EMS experience. Roman had eighteen years of EMS experience in the New York City area and was what most EMS workers would call 'burned out', from the approximately fifteen thousand calls he responded to during that time. More than half of the calls were not remotely considered life-threatening calls and merely boiled down to transportation, or EMS cab rides, to the hospital without any medical treatment being applied except to check vital signs. Roman frequently bristled and grumbled about responding to the "bullshit" calls. On this call he was already grumbling about the drivers on the road not getting out of the way for an emergency vehicle with lights and sirens on. "Come on asshole, how can you NOT see these bright red flashing lights in your rear view mirror - in the middle of the night?"

Dexter, on the other hand, was somewhat seasoned, but, still fairly new to the New York City EMS experience. He still had the enjoyment and desire to want to help others. He still had an appetite for emergency medicine and constantly wanted to learn more. He was one hundred percent certain that medical school was in his future because he knew he wanted more than an EMT or paramedic career. As they maneuvered around traffic, his mind was recalling the NYS protocol for delivering babies.

Newlin's EMS experience was questionable, at best. Volunteer ambulance experience in the suburbs, compared to NYC ambulance experience, was like comparing a bicycle with training wheels to a Harley-Davidson motorcycle. His face exposed an inner conflict of excitement versus terror going on inside of him. He sat in the back of the ambulance trying to give off a cool, composed projection, but his body language projected nervousness, and possibly fright, like a deer caught in a car's headlights. "Do you guys deliver a lot of babies in the Bronx?"

"Yeah, about once a month, and we haven't had one for this month yet," recalled Roman.

While Dexter's mind was running through the NYS EMT protocol for treating pregnant women and the possible complications that might occur, Roman was grumbling. "Why tie up an ambulance to take your pregnant wife to the hospital? The husband should waddle her fat ass down to the car, or a cab, and drive her to the hospital himself. That's what I did with all of my kids. And why do these women wait to the damn last minute?"

RICO HAD WINED AND DINED HER. Now, as they entered her apartment, he was going to get a little Puerto Rican dessert. They had rocked boots before and Rico found her to be an energetic and passionate sex partner. The sex was off the Richter scale on the prior occasion. He felt that he was in great shape and on top of his game, and expected more of the same from her tonight. He loved the Taino Indian coloring of her skin and the full voluptuous curves of her breasts and hips, complimenting her small thin waist. Everything about her was a turn-on.

She usually hid her body behind a baggy nurse's uniform at the hospital, but she couldn't hide the beauty of her smile and features, nor the charm and sexiness that poured through her skin.

"Do you want something to drink?" she asked as she turned on some music from a CD player.

"Sure, Eve. What do you have? I'm sorry. Evelyn, do you mind that I call you Eve?"

"No. I don't mind at all," she smiled a smile that made him melt, then came over and kissed him gently. "I'll be your Eve. Does that mean you want some apple wine?" she smiled that smile again.

"You are a rare breed, Eve. Most Puerto Rican women your age in the Bronx are working on their fourth kid and their second husband, with plenty of angry, jealous baby-daddy drama mixed in. How did you escape?"

She handed him a glass of wine. "I had the protection of four older brothers that everyone in the neighborhood was afraid of. My oldest brother nearly beat some guy to death for playfully grabbing me around my waist. I wasn't able to escape them until I started nursing school, at a college miles away from home."

"Remind me to never go to your family barbeque. "

"It's safe at home now. One brother is dead, one is in jail, one works for the transit authority and you know my other brother Roman, on the ambulance."

"Roman Reyes is your brother?"

"He's the youngest of my four older brothers. I've seen you two talking. He says he knows you, but that's all he ever says, he knows you."

Rico was a little surprised. He didn't like to mix business and pleasure. Eve's relationship to Roman could complicate matters, and he wasn't sure he felt comfortable with the situation. However, he didn't want to stop seeing Eve. She was a special woman in many ways. He would have to think this out, long and hard. In the meantime this drop-dead gorgeous woman with an hour-glass figure and six-figure salaried job was sitting on the couch a foot away with a drink in her hand. He couldn't have imagined this scene in his wildest dreams while in prison. The memories of sleeping on prison gym floors, bland food, freezing cells at night, being locked-up in 'the hole' for fighting, and the constant threats, harassment and tension to always be on guard and watch ones back, all seemed like another lifetime ago.

Rico raised his glass. Eve raised her glass. "Here's to the beginning of something wonderfully special," toasted Rico. They touched glasses, looked into each other's eyes and drank.

Rico put his glass down. Eve put her glass down also. Rico took both of her hands in his, held them and studied them. Soft, perfectly feminine, yet not weak. He kissed them gently, moving his kisses slowly up her forearms to her upper arms. He slid closer to her then he moved his lips from her shoulder across to her neck and then down the cleavage of her dress. Even her perfume was sensuous and perfect, he thought. Her moans gave him approval to continue.

As he gently slid his body on top of her, she put her hand on his chest to stop him.

Surprised, Rico looked up at her face. She smiled and maneuvered out from under him. As she got up from the couch, she took his hand and led him to the bedroom. Her dress gently caressing her swaying hips while some singer was crooning about the wonders of sexual healing from the CD player. She walked with a slow, naturally sensuous, rhythm. Almost a subdued runway model's flair. It always amazed him that many beautiful women walked like gorillas or cave dwellers, without the slightest trace of grace or balance. Rico couldn't tell if her erotic walk was natural or taught, but it was hypnotic to watch.

She stopped at the queen-sized bed, then slowly, effortlessly took off her dress revealing a matching black bra and thong set. "I'll be right back," she purred as she walked to a small bathroom next to the bedroom. Although he had seen her body before, he was still awestruck as though he were seeing it for the first time.

Rico sat on the bed and took off his shoes. She returned within moments wearing only a black sheer thigh-length nightgown. Now it was Rico's turn as she dimmed the lights and crawled into bed. He began to strip down to his boxers, deliberately flexing his chest, lats and abdominal muscles as he pulled his undershirt over his head. Although he was considered to be average height, he knew he had a better than average body. Rico felt that the benefit of prison, if there is such a thing as a benefit of prison, was that the regimented days and boxing training had firmly developed his upper body and his stamina. Even now, nearly one year out of prison, his body still was chiseled and rock hard with only twice a week workouts at the gym as maintenance.

He knew she was watching and enjoying the show, but he didn't want to take too long. He took off his boxer shorts and quickly folded them, laying them on top of his already folded trousers and shirt. All the while facing Eve and letting her absorb the full view of his body, using every opportunity to get her further excited. He was proud of his body, even proud of his battle wounds: an abdominal stab wound while fighting in juvenile jail, and a gunshot wound to the lower back that miraculously missed vital organs, a year before going to prison.
Rico crawled into the bed with Eve, laying a few inches away from her. She reached over and gently stroked his well-

defined chest muscles, then his ripped abs and, finally, she gasped momentarily, as she stroked his erection.

"Now, where were we?" asked Rico, as he leaned over and began kissing her neck and breasts. He felt her lips gently kissing the top of his head and her fingers running through his hair, her other hand was pulling him closer to her. He laid his head on her left breast, with his ear directly above her heart, while kissing and caressing her right breast. He could hear her heart racing a mile a minute, while the moans were becoming more frequent. Her excitement was stimulating him even more.

RICO CRUISED ALONG THE HIGHWAY on his way to the office for a Saturday morning meeting with Steven Spellman. Spellman wanted to strategize the Angel Rivera case, the little girl that fell out the fourth floor apartment window, but Rico was already ahead of the game. He had done his research and investigation into some of the details of the case. He knew that Spellman, like many lawyers, was primarily interested in the monetary value of the case and the likelihood of winning.

After marathon sex with Eve last night, followed by a morning encore, a shower and her home cooked breakfast with strong Spanish coffee, Rico felt ready to take on Spellman and the world. The sun and the cool fresh morning air felt invigorating coming through the open sunroof and windows. Life was good. Damn good.

Pulling into the law office parking lot Rico saw Spellman's Jag in his usual parking space. Rico glanced at his watch. He was early and Spellman was even earlier.

DEXTER AND NEWBY WALKED FROM the Emergency Room to the ambulance bay at the rear entrance of the hospital. Roman had disappeared with a nurse's aid, and probably screwed her in the storage closet of the hospital.

"Dave, that was a typical and routine call. It appears that this woman was unsure if she was pregnant and really wanted the ER to give her a free pregnancy test. Do you have any questions about the call, or the company, or questions about anything?"

"Well my first question, is Roman busting my chops or is he always like this with all new guys?"

"Don't let Roman frazzle you. He's a good guy, just a little burnt after fifteen years of doing this kind of stuff. It has a tendency to burn people out, the constant adrenaline pump of flying to calls that are perceived to be life-threatening with lights and sirens, but many of those same calls turn out to be non-emergencies. He has a theory that he calls the PIE theory."

"The PIE theory? What is that, like the Pythagorean math equation, Pi squared?"

"No," laughed Dexter. "Roman feels that approximately seventy to eighty percent of the ambulance calls here in the South Bronx fall into the PIE category. These are calls that aren't real emergencies at all, but the caller calls the 9-1-1 systems because the caller is either, 'Poor, Ignorant or Elderly.' P.I.E."

"He feels that the poor call 911, because they can't afford health insurance and don't have a primary physician. They use the ER as a doctor's office, for example, because a teenage child has a cold. Medicaid pays for everything including the ambulance, the ER and the prescription meds. Why should they pay for a cab or sit in the waiting area for hours when they can call 9-1-1 and get a free ride to the ER and get pushed to the front of the waiting line?"

"The medically ignorant call 911, because they don't have a general understanding of the human body. A new mother will call 9-1-1 because the four month old won't stop crying for thirty minutes in the middle of the night and they think the baby has a fever. When asked if they changed, fed, burped the baby, or took a temperature, they say no."

"I don't agree with all of his theory, especially with regard to the elderly, but I understand his frustration with the abuse of the EMS system in New York City. We had a patient the other night who, after waiting four hours in the Emergency Room without being seen, walked outside to the corner, called 911 on a payphone, and when we arrived asked to be taken to another Emergency Room across town because he was tired of waiting so long."

"Roman must have flipped on the guy," smiled Newlin.

"We handled it as professionally as possible, and without incident," replied Dexter guardedly.

"You told me about Roman's PIE theory; what's your theory of Bronx EMS?"

"I feel that he and I differ because of where we are on the time and experience spectrum. I'm young and I'm a people person. I like people, generally, and genuinely enjoy helping others, especially the very old and the very young. To me, that should be one of the prerequisites to being in the medical field. It shouldn't only be about money or status; it should be about helping others. I know that's a little naïve and unrealistic, but that's how I feel."

"I think that people in careers where there is constant stress and adrenalin surges, like PD and EMS, tend to burn out after years of exposure to the stress and that type of environment. After a while they feel that every call is a false call or outright abuse, as soon as it comes across the radio. That's where Roman is at the intersection of, but he is still one of the best EMTs around," continued Dexter, "but what about you, Dave? What is your theory of EMS? Why are you here?"

"I dunno, I guess you could say that I'm here to learn things," shrugged Newlin, as Roman walked up to them smiling, after a romp in a closet.

CHAPTER

9

AS THEY PULLED UP to the scene with flashing emergency lights brightening the night- darkened street, Roman grumbled some more. This time about the family member waving frantically from the front steps of the building. "Alright, we see you and your damn iridescent shirt," he mumbled barely audible to himself.

A teenage looking male with a rainbow colored tee shirt approached them, "You have to hurry, the baby is coming out." He then dashed inside the building to alert the others.

Roman looked at Newlin, sitting in the opening between the front cab and rear patient compartment, and smiled, "I love it. Baptism by fire. Finally, we get a chance to see what you're made of, Newby. I'll bet it's nothing like what you get on the Long Island suburbs."

They grabbed their equipment and started up the stairs to the second floor apartment, just as a police car pulled up next to their ambulance. Upon entering the sparsely furnished apartment they found a sea of humanity in what appeared to be the living room leading to a bedroom. "Excuse me, EMS coming through," said Roman in Spanish, as they took hurried steps toward the rhythmic screaming coming from the bedroom. The sea of humanity parted. A half dozen kids, a half dozen middle-aged women and a few middle-aged men comprised the first layer of people squeezed around the entry door to the small bedroom.

Once inside the 10-foot by 10-foot bedroom, they found a few more women surrounding the mother. The room had only a twin-sized mattress with box spring on the floor against a wall and a small cheap six-drawer dresser against another wall. The two windows in the room were covered with plain white bed sheets nailed above the windows and hanging loosely to the ground, while a rope clothes-line with more sheets on it also served as a privacy wall separating the room into not quite two halves.

Roman ushered the women out the room and he closed the door, to give the patient privacy. He asked the police officers to keep everyone out. Dexter stepped to the foot of the bed to assess the situation. The young woman suddenly began screaming again in a high-pitched voice, and with every muscle in her body tensed, clutched the edges of the mattress in a vise-tight grip. She was laying on her back with a small puddle of clear fluids between her bent, wide-open legs on the bed, evidence to Dexter that apparently the amniotic sac had ruptured and delivery might be immediate. The screaming stopped momentarily and the mother was panting forcefully.

"Hello, Mom. How are you doing so far?" asked Dexter. She nodded okay as she continued panting, while beads of perspiration ran down her face to her neck.

"Alright, Mom. You are going to be okay," he reassured her. "How many weeks pregnant are you, or when are you due?"

She mumbled, "Yesterday."

"How many babies do you have?"

She held up two fingers.

Again she let out a scream and began panting. The contractions were getting closer and closer together, less than two minutes apart, noted Dexter, and apparently stronger.

"That's okay, just breathe. Take deep breaths, in and out through your mouth. You are doing fine."

"I have to check to see where the baby is," said Dexter as he donned gloves, but standing at the foot of the mattress he could already see crowning, the perineum was bulging significantly, and the top of the infant's head was visible at the vaginal opening.

Roman gloved up, then broke open an OB/GYN kit and quickly began to prepare the delivery field, using sheets from the obstetric kit. He placed one under her buttocks, one over her abdomen and one long sheet behind her back with either end draped over her thighs.

Looking around, Dexter spotted Newlin standing motionless up against the closed door looking like he was in a hypnotic trance and about to pass out. "Hey Dave, can you try and get some vitals on the mother for me and just record the time of birth on our paperwork when she delivers, okay?"

Dave nodded acknowledgement, but he didn't move otherwise, and his eyes never left the woman, or the miracle of nature that he was witnessing about to emerge from her womb.

"Dave! Today! Before the kid hits puberty," growled Roman. The forcefulness and urgency in his voice caught the rookie's attention and snapped him back into focus. He walked over to the equipment bag and took out a blood pressure cuff.

The woman screamed loudly again, "Aieee, it's coming, I have to push."

Dexter kneeled down on the mattress at the mother's ankles and observed the little head of the infant slowly emerge from the vaginal opening, face down, coming out further and further with each contraction. The mother's screams were at their loudest, as he tried to encourage and reassure her. "You're doing great momma, just keep taking deep breaths through your mouth and push." He took his gloved hand and supported the head, while trying to ensure that there was no explosive delivery and also ensuring that the umbilical cord wasn't wrapped around the infant's neck. Roman, on cue, handed him the suction bulb and Dexter suctioned fluids from the mouth then nostrils of the infant.

The rest of the delivery went well.

Dexter picked up the baby with gloved hands from the pool of birthing fluids on the bed and noticed that the afterbirth hadn't delivered. The long gray-blue umbilical cord went from the newborn's belly to the mother's vaginal opening and disappeared into the mother's vagina. The baby's color was good, his breathing rate was good and his pulse rate was also good. Dexter lightly plucked the baby's foot with his finger, which caused the desired result, an immediate and healthy cry.

"Hey Dave, come over here for a minute," called Roman. "Since this is your first delivery, you've been selected to cut the umbilical cord. Maybe if you do a good job, mama here will name the baby after you." Roman took two clamps and a scalpel out of the OB/GYN kit, handing the covered scalpel to Dave as he applied the two clamps at the appropriate spots on the umbilical cord. "Okay Dave, you're gonna cut between the two clamps."

Dave stepped forward and looked at the umbilical cord. One end was attached to the precious little new life that had entered this world, and the other end traveled up and disappeared into the bushy vagina of the mother and into her womb. Dave tried to keep his composure and keep his hand from trembling uncontrollably. The last thing he remembered was how hot it was in the apartment and how he had just witnessed one of life's miracles, the birth of a child, the beginning of life, and he didn't want to screw it up.

Roman readied a special futuristic looking silver blanket to help the baby retain his heat and keep him warm, after being in the mother's 98.7 degree womb for the past nine months. Dexter placed the baby in the blanket. Roman wrapped him and placed him in the mother's arms. "Little man is built like a future lineman for the New York Jets."

"You had a little boy, momma. Doesn't appear that you've lost more than the usual amount of blood, so just keep taking deep breaths and rubbing your belly. I'm gonna check your little boy, then we're going to wait a few minutes for the afterbirth and leave for the hospital."

DEXTER SIGNED OUT AND WALKED to his car, saying good-bye as Roman ragged on Dave.

"Yeah, it was pretty obvious that it was your first delivery, Newby. What's not obvious is whether you passed out because of witnessing the delivery, or because it was your first close-up encounter with a real, live vagina. But don't worry, after a few months in the South Bronx you'll be able to categorize 'em: short, fat, skinny, long, hideous, or beautiful. They run the scale," howled Roman.

Newlin stood there in the South Bronx Ambulance garage grinning sheepishly. Moments after the delivery, he woke up on a couch in the patient's apartment with an old woman wiping his brow with a wet cloth that reeked of rubbing alcohol and two NYPD cops grinning at him.

"I guess where you volunteer on Long Island, the chauffer or maid drives the pregnant mom to the hospital. Right?"

"How did I get from the bedroom to the couch in the other room?"

"Luckily, you passed out and fell backwards with the scalpel cover still on. We left you on the floor for a few minutes, until the mother delivered the afterbirth. You started to come around by then, so we got the two cops to help you out of the room and sit you on a couch. We thought we were gonna have three patients for a minute. At least you provided a source of laughter and amusement for the mother and family. I'm sure the cops will pass the story on to the other cops in the precinct, you are gonna be famous, or should I say, infamous."

Dexter reached his car and unlocked the door.

"Where's the damn "S" and cape?" growled a voice in the parked car behind him.

"Hey, O'Neal. Whazup? How was last night for you guys?"

"Nothing like you guys lately, with kids out of window, front page of the newspapers and now delivering babies. You guys are getting more attention than the mayor of New York City."

"Yeah, but it ain't putting more dollars in my pocket. Though it does feel kinda good."

"My teenaged niece saw the front page picture and thinks you're kinda cute. She asked me to get your autograph. I told her that kind of talk would get her a smack in the mouth."

Dexter didn't ask, but he felt that O'Neal's teenaged niece would get smacked in the mouth for drooling over a man, any man. Himmler's teenaged daughter, if he had one, would get smacked in the mouth for drooling over a 'black' man. He chuckled and opened the trunk of his car.

It had been a good night in the South Bronx. One newborn delivery, a few of the usual generic stomach/head ache sick calls, a motor vehicle accident, and Pedro, the neighborhood drunk, who had a seizure inside of a Spanish restaurant. Dexter was headed to the track next to Yankee Stadium for his bi-weekly two-mile jog. Then he would head home, shower and fix a couple of sandwiches, get water, towels, sun block, MP3 player, and a book, then head to Orchard Beach for a few hours of Bronx sun. And, maybe he would shoot some hoops if some of the good players were there.

He thought about calling his girlfriend, Josette, and asking her to join him, but figured it was short notice and she probably had to work today. Facially, she was an average looking light-brown skinned woman with a thick body, but she had a bubbly, spirited, happy personality with an infectious laugh. He enjoyed her intellect, being around her, and felt it wasn't only about the sex. He also enjoyed her independence; she had a high paying administrative job, a nice apartment and a luxury car, that she barely used. She was a big hearted, generous soul to many of her students and causes, but she was especially generous to Dexter, lavishing him with extravagant gifts, which he sometimes felt awkward accepting. He felt uneasy about the gifts because he wasn't always able to reciprocate with gifts of equal value, and he certainly didn't want Josette to ever feel that he was using her for her material gain.

It was now a good morning. The sun was out and a warm gentle breeze was stirring the aromas of the South Bronx through the parking lot. The smell of bread and pastries from a local Spanish bakery dominated the air, mightily overpowering the stench of rotted overflowing garbage, discarded rice and beans with chicken wings on the curbs, half empty bottles of beer in the gutters, and the occasional canine excrement on the streets and sidewalks.

He threw his workbag in the back of his ten-year-old mid-sized Ford and pulled out of the SoBro Ambulance parking lot.

RICO SAT IN SPELLMAN'S OFFICE, while Spellman and his wife chatted off in a corner about something regarding their pool. They finished up and walked arm in arm toward Rico sitting in front of Spellman's desk. Rico couldn't remember seeing him this pleasant and happy. But the past several months were very busy and lucrative, maybe his most lucrative ever.

"Rico, Mrs. Spellman and I are having a party at our house next weekend. We are extending an invitation to you and a guest. We hope you and your guest will honor us with your presence. Weather permitting, it will be an outdoor causal BBQ style affair. The pool will be open, there will be live entertainment and the crowd will be a mix of lawyers, judges, business people, entertainers, and of course my friends and family. You have been a very pleasant addition to the firm and as you know I follow the credo of 'work hard, play hard.'"

Rico tried not to show his surprise at the invitation. He was being invited into the fringes of Spellman's inner circle. They had gotten closer over the past months, and Spellman didn't come off as irritating and obnoxious as he did during the first few months of Rico's employment, however, Rico didn't see this coming. An invitation to Spellman's house for a party during the first months would have conjured up images of Rico being asked to serve as a valet or bartender, to which he would have politely declined.

"Thank you, Mr. Spellman. I would be happy to attend."

"With a guest?"

"Yes, I have someone I've been dating. I'll see if she's available."

"Great. Bring swimming suits; the pool will be open and heated. Now that that is settled and out of the way, let us get down to business," said Spellman sitting behind his desk. His wife silently walked to and out of the office door closing it quietly. She avoided eye contact with Rico and he avoided eye contact with her.

"First, I have an errand for you to run on Monday. I have a case that has just passed its date to file notice with the opposing insurance company. I have a contact in the post office that I want you to take the envelope to. My contact will postdate the U.S. postage date to make it legit. I will give you the particulars before you leave today. Of course, this is just between you and me. Is that understood?"

"Next, talk to me about the Angel Rivera case. What information have you discovered during your research and investigation?"

"Originally, I thought this was a slam-dunk case. However, it's now starting to get shaky. The owner is carrying a half million dollar liability policy on a twenty apartment-unit building. While the New York Window-Guard Laws require landlords to provide window guards in apartments where children ten years of age or younger reside, a landlord is not liable for falls from unguarded windows unless the child was a "resident" of the apartment unit. The courts have held that owners are not liable for children falling from unguarded windows when the child was a guest and did not reside in the apartment. Right now, it is unclear if the mother is the renter on record. Furthermore, it appears that the mother is a crack addict, and my informants tell me on the night of the accident she left the apartment to buy drugs."

"That poor kid. I expect you to continue your research and investigatory work into this case, and keep me posted as soon as you find anything, negative or positive. Have you Sheppardized the facts of the case yet?"

"I'm still working on it."

"YOU KNOW THAT ROOKIES are supposed to pay for coffee for the first week, right?" asked Roman. The three of them ordered a round of coffee and donuts from the Dunkin Donuts location on Third Avenue, on their way to their coverage area. It was something of a tradition with Dexter and Roman, getting coffee around two or three in the morning as a boost, or re-fueling, for the second half of the midnight tour. They viewed it almost the same as lunch for the 9-5 crowd.

"I don't know about for the week, but I got it covered today," grinned Dave. "Tell me something. Why do you two guys stay in this line of work? It seems it has a lot of negatives."

"I've been doing this type of work for eighteen years. Yeah, there are nights when we get our butts kicked, but those nights are rare. There are just as many nights when we get no-hitters. To me it's easy work, its stable work and the pay puts food on the table. The healthcare industry is almost recession-proof. Except for recession periods, you ain't gonna hear about too many hospitals or ambulance services shutting down. Also, it gives me flexibility. It's a 24-hour a day, 365 days of the year gig. I can pick my hours. I can work nights here, days somewhere else or hustle, doing evenings at another place. I teach CPR on the side and make extra cash off the books, because of the flexibility I have from here," said Roman.

"Yeah, I see your point."

"Besides, one of the perks of the job is all the ass you meet. Hospital staff, patients with good looking family members, female NYPD, even pedestrians walking down the street, or in the stores." As Roman spoke, he nodded toward the woman behind the counter bending over to reach the donuts. She looked Hispanic, in her thirties, with a medium brown, thick and firm body. The tight black pants she was wearing seemed to stretch even tighter around her buttocks as they flexed during her stretch for the donuts, and the panty line became more pronounced. Her Dunkin Donuts golf shirt revealed a lot of bosom bursting over the unbuttoned top. Roman mouthed the word "H-O-T-T-Y" to Dave.

"Yes, I truly see your point," said Dave as he noticed the few other male patrons in the store gazing at the tightly clad counter-girl who made every movement seem like soft-core-porn.

"What about you, Dex?"

"I still don't know what I wanna be when I grow up," chuckled Dexter, "but I enjoy this work right now. I enjoy the medical field and I enjoy helping people, interacting with people. I think that is what you need to do this kind of work. And I agree with Romie about this being a flexible job. I can work nights and go to school during the day or evening."

"What about the pay?"

"The pay sucks. When janitors and secretaries are making more than the paramedics who save lives, then you know there's a problem. I mean, no disrespect to janitors and secretaries, God bless 'em, but when you consider the training and certifications required to become an EMT or paramedic, and that often there are lives at stake, things are a little skewed.   Luckily for me, I don't have a wife and kids, but things are even tight for me on a full-time salary."

Roman began to engage the counter-girl in conversation, in Spanish. Dave handed her a ten-dollar bill. She responded smilingly and easily to Roman's banter.

As they walked out of the brightly lit Dunkin Donuts onto the dimly lit night streets, "See what I mean Dave, about plenty of ass from this job? Her name is Maria. She's Dominican and gets off at eight in the morning. I told her I'd pick her up. But you know what the funny thing is? Part of the attraction is this uniform and the ambulance, which means I got a well-paying job, or so the women think."

"Yo rook, you want me to see if she's got a friend? Nah, never mind. You ain't ready yet. I give you another five or six months in the Bronx. Then maybe..." razzed Roman to Newby. "To me, Dominican women are some of the most beautiful women in the world. Especially from the age of about sixteen to twenty-eight. After they spit out a few kids they puff up big time. When they're young they have a beautiful brown caramel skin that is a blend of genes between African slaves and white Spaniards. Their bodies are firm, thick and extremely well developed, they remind me of amazons from the jungle. I used to work on an ambulance stationed in 'little Dominica' on 180 Street and Broadway in upper Manhattan. I needed ball-bearings in my neck to watch all the Dominican women, almost bursting out of their clothes, while they walked up and down the street. They would just be wearing jeans and a tee shirt without any makeup, but they had a natural beauty that made them look better than some of the star actresses and models you see in the movies, with all of their caked on make-up."

"Hey Roman," asked Newby, "is your name really Roman, or is that a nickname?"

"That's the real deal. The story my mother tells is that my father went to give the hospital my name and sign the birth certificate, but when the big breasted clerk bent over the desk my father got distracted and turned R-A-M-O-N into R-O-M-A-N."

"My father tells the story that he was so drunk from celebrating the birth of another son that when he went to sign the papers he got a mental block and forgot how to spell Ramon. So whether you want to blame it on big tits or alcohol, I am forever known as Roman."

"Or Romeo, as we sometimes call him," added Dexter.

CHAPTER

10

DEXTER SAT AT A SMALL two seat lunchroom table in Morrisania Community College, diagonally across from two young female college students talking at another small two-seat table. He had taken the night off from work and was there for an EMS Continuing Medical Education seminar that dealt with EMS Trauma. Dexter was attending because he was interested in trauma calls and because the doctor giving the lecture was a past NYC paramedic whom he knew and admired. Dr. Malcolm Elliot Dickerson was a humble, but sharp prodigy who worked his way up from ambulance driver to EMT - to paramedic - to medical doctor. In a very short time he became Medical Director of a small Bronx hospital's Emergency Department, within walking distance of the community college. Dexter looked at Malcolm as a big brother, mentor and friend of whom he could ask questions and pick his brains about medicine, medical school, politics, sports or any subject, really.

They had agreed to meet in the cafeteria after the lecture was over. The seminar was unusually crowded, but had the usual post lecture friends, acquaintances and hanger-ons that wanted to meet, rub elbows and talk at length with the guest lecturer. Dexter knew that Malcolm would generously and politely talk to those that hung around after, so he came down to the cafeteria to get a tuna sandwich and iced tea.

He liked this cafeteria. The layout was clever, mildly colorful, but most of all, it was exceptionally clean. The prices were reasonable and the food was good; that didn't hurt either. Further evidence of the quality of the cafeteria was the fact that several suit-types were seated in booths against the walls. Dexter made a mental note to stop by for lunch or dinner on his day off to check it out further. Suddenly his cellphone rang. A quick peek at the caller ID showed that it was Roman.

"Whazup, Romie? Did that Dominican wear you out old man?"

"Yo D, man this is serious shit. You alone? Can you talk?" asked Roman.

"Yeah, I'm alone. What's up?" asked Dexter sensing the stress in Romie's voice.

"I can't fucking believe this. I was called and asked to come in early. As soon as I get there I get called into the office. Bob gives me this sealed envelope from the IG's office in Manhattan. I open the shit and it's a letter telling me to report to an investigatory hearing in two days, regarding some alleged criminal actions on my part."

"Wait. Slow down. Who, and what is the I G?"

Dexter strained to hear the words over the distant clattering of dishes, cups, silverware and talking from the dinner crowd in the background. "The IG. The Inspector General's office. They are responsible for the investigation and elimination of corruption, criminal activity, conflict of interest, and unethical conduct by people or businesses doing business with the City. You know, stuff like Medicaid fraud and NYC Housing Authority rip offs," exclaimed Roman.

"So do you have any idea what this is about?"

"None at all. The only remote thing could be the hook up with the lawyer's office and the motor vehicle accidents, but that's like getting called into court for flicking boogers. I don't get it."

"Do you think you should contact your friend at the lawyer's office and ask him?"

"Nah. Not yet. I'll save that as my trump card until I know for sure what this is all about. For all I know they could have me mixed up with one of the other fifty thousand Puerto Ricans named Reyes in New York. But in the meantime, I am temporarily suspended from doing patient care work at SoBro Ambulance, pending the outcome of this investigatory hearing."

DEXTER ARRIVED AT WORK the next night with Romie's situation on his mind and expecting his partner would be David Newlin for the period of Charlie's suspension. However, he didn't see Newlin's car in the SoBro parking lot. As he walked past the ambulance garage doors, Supervisor Bob summoned him to the office.

"Dexter, I have been ordered to give you this letter," said Bob, handing him a sealed white business envelope. In the return address corner was typed Office of the Inspector General.

Dexter looked at Bob's face, who averted eye contact. Dexter looked around to make sure the office was clear. He then walked over to the glass door and closed it.

"Off the record, what the fuck is going on?"

"What did you and Roman do?" said Bob sadly shaking his head. "Off the record, people I know say it looks like the IG was investigating Medicaid and insurance fraud, when it got wind of some shyster lawyers and doctors doing auto insurance scams, with the help of some hospital and ambulance employees."

Dexter started to walk out of the office when Bob said, "Listen I'm sorry, but I gotta tell you that the boss says, for legal and liability reasons, you're suspended from doing patient care at SoBro, pending the outcome of this investigation. Once you're cleared, you can come back to work."

Anger, confusion and rage were all competing for a voice, so rather than tell Bob, the messenger, to go fuck himself, Dexter just walked out of the office.

He walked back to his car; his mind racing. He sat in his car with the sole parking lot lamppost giving off the faintest of light in the night. He put on his car's interior light and read the letter several times, incredulously. Why was he implicated? What should he say? Should he deny any knowledge? Does Romie know, and what will he say?

"Romie, can you meet me somewhere?" asked Dexter over his cell phone.

"Yeah, whazup?"

"I just got the same IG letter at work."

"What? You're fucking with me, right?"

"No, I'm dead serious. We have to meet and talk."

"Okay, I'm was just leaving the Dominican's apartment in upper Manhattan. Let's meet at the coffee shop next to Yankee Stadium."

Dexter made it there in fifteen minutes and waited another fifteen minutes for Romie, taking a booth in the back, facing the front door. The coffee shop front entrance was on East 161st Street, one block east of Yankee Stadium and one block west of the Bronx Courthouse, with a large glass window next to the door. The layout at the front of the shop was a ten foot long counter running from the front to almost the back of the shop, behind which lay assorted trays of donuts on multiple shelves, coffee machines and a cash register ten feet from the door. Another counter, with stools propped like metal soldiers on one side for patron seating, led to the back. At the back of the coffee shop, were booths and small tables, and an opening where the counter-help entered and exited the counter.

If the three most important factors to the marketing experts is "location, location and location," then the shop was in marketing heaven, thought Dexter. Besides its proximity to the stadium and the courthouse, it was also one block from the elevated 4 train line and the D underground subway. About six different bus lines stopped near the corner and fed passengers into the train lines and received passengers from the train lines. It made for a nearly constant flow of customers into the coffee shop, most of whom stopped at the front counter and got coffee with donuts or sandwiches to take out.

Romie entered looking fresh, showered and clean-shaven. He was wearing a white custom-made button up shirt, with designer jeans and shiny black loafers. He slid into the opposite bench facing Dexter.

"Even in times of stress, you're out chasing ass. You are unbelievable."

"That's funny, the Dominican said I was unbelievable too. Taurus, the bull, baby," grinned Roman waving the waitress over. "You want a coffee?"

"No, I'm jittery enough. I had two already."

RICO AND EVELYN were led through the home to the side of the house where there was an expansive patio area with a large pool and a tennis court. It was a warm sunny Saturday afternoon, with not a cloud in the sky. The smoky aroma of BBQ chicken, steak kabobs, hot dogs and burgers billowed gently over the small gathering of approximately seventy-five people.

Everything about Spellman's home in Westchester County New York whispered money, as one would expect from a county that had one of the highest property taxes in the country. It also befits a community that boasts: its' residents were a past United States President and another was a past United States Senator. Plushness and lavishness whispered from the exotic Italian tiles on the ground of the 25-foot by 25-foot outdoor patio, to the outdoor kitchen island with a top of the line BBQ grille-oven-sink- fridge set-up. Even the dozen or so hired help looked and sounded like they were borrowed from the British Royal Kingdom for the day. No high school/college kids, nor minimum wage immigrants for Spellman. Only the best professional help around, thought Rico.

The large grassy area around the patio and pool looked as if it were expecting a round of golf to start any minute. Each blade of grass appeared to have been perfectly and individually cut.

The pool was clean and spotless, reflecting the bright sky off its waters, with several bamboo-wicker recliners and tables with chairs ensembles scattered around poolside. It appeared to have Olympic dimensions and was being used only by an elderly couple and a pair that appeared in their mid-fifties. A moderately sized hot tub was situated ten feet away from one end of the pool.

"Glad you could make it, Rico," said Spellman walking toward them with a drink in his hand.

Rico turned and faced him. Spellman put out his hand and they shook. Spellman was wearing a pair of khaki shorts, a colorful Hawaiian print short-sleeve shirt, sandals and a wide brim Caribbean-style straw hat.

"Love the hat," smiled Rico.

"A souvenir from St. Bart's last summer."

"Mr. Spellman, this is Evelyn Reyes. Evelyn, this is Steven Spellman."

"Ah, yes. The young prince's princess. Enchanted," said the smiling, charming Spellman. "It is a pleasure and delight to meet you. Rico has an exquisite eye for pulchritude."

Evelyn smiled and did a mini curtsey toward Spellman, who in turn did a slight distinguished gentleman's bow at the waist.

"If you two brought swimming suits, would you please put them on and liven up the pool area for me? You can change in the cabana over there next to the pool. I have to go talk to the band to pick up the pace. It's starting to sound like a funeral out here."

"We have them on already."

Rico and Eve walked over to recliners beside the middle of the pool. They sat and removed their outer clothes and laid them on tables next to the recliners. While pulling his golf shirt over his head, he looked up from his chair to the standing Eve, who was pulling her hair back into a pony tail. His face was level with her navel. The sun hit her waist at such an angle as to reveal a natural and magnificently bronzed six-pack, the beauty of which almost took his breath away. She had on a modest gold colored two-piece swimsuit that accentuated her hourglass figure. The bottom piece had a two-inch opening on either side that was connected by two gold hoops. The top piece also had a two-inch opening at mid-chest that connected the two sides with two miniature golden hoops. He had never seen her body in the full sunlight, only during late night and early morning bedroom sessions. It was even more impressive in the sunlight, as he watched the muscles of her legs and hips gracefully glide her over to the edge of the pool.

He watched her step into the pool but was aware that he wasn't the only one watching. One of the male servers with a tray of beer was observing her, as were a few of the other male guests in the patio area; a few were sneaking hidden peaks while a few seemed to be outright drooling.

As he scanned the crowd, he noticed a pair of eyes devouring him. Michelle Spellman was sitting at a crowded table on the patio listening and entertaining a small group of five. She was situated in a chair that was facing in the direction of the pool and allowed her to occasionally glance at those at poolside. Rico realized that she was getting a good view of his body and was impressed by his build, based on the frequency of her glances. He got up from his chair and slowly walked over to the pool, watching Eve as she swam a few laps, then got in.

DEXTER HANDED the receptionist the letter.

She read the front sheet and smiled, "Mr. Reed, please have a seat. I'll advise Mr. Goldstein that you are here. Will you be having legal representation at the hearing?"

"No."

"Okay. That's fine. I have to ask."

Dexter and Romie had discussed their strategy at the coffee shop. Romie wanted Dexter to deny any knowledge of Romie's activities, to avoid any penalties or charges being thrown at his friend. Romie might give them crumbs to see what they knew, but he wanted to force them to prove what they knew. Their strategy was to 'feel-the-IG-out' for the first round.

It never occurred to him to bring an attorney to the hearing, although it was mentioned in the letter. Not that he could afford one, but since the secretary mentioned it, it made him concerned about how serious this hearing was going to be.

He sat in the small waiting area of the office across from the receptionist and a couple steps from the four elevators. There was a long hall behind the receptionist's desk, the first of which had 'Conference Room' printed on its door. As he sat there, he thought about the exchange he had when he entered the lobby of the building.

After waiting on a security checkpoint line for five minutes, Dexter reached the search area. First, he had to empty his pockets and take off his watch and necklace. Then, after going through the metal detector three times, and it alarming each time he went through, followed by a uniformed big, black female with a serious attitude waving a wand over his clothing, a diminutive Latino woman with lieutenant's bars on her white shirt collar walked over.

Her facial skin looked leathery tough and she had a short Cesar-style haircut with shocking white hair. "What's the problem?" she asked, looking Dexter up and down with obvious disdain. "If we can't correct this here, then we have to take you in our office and have you undress, if you want to go into this building. Do you have anything metal that you are hiding?" Although she was half the size of the black woman, she had ten times the attitude and gave the impression that she was either an ex-marine or an ex-Bronx resident.

The line that he was in had stopped moving due to this occurrence and Dexter could hear grumbling behind him. He noticed a few of the male security officers watching him from their stations at other metal detectors.

She took the metal detector wand from the big, black woman and passed it slowly over different areas of Dexter's body. This is ridiculous, he thought. He felt like just walking out and going back home. Suddenly the wand started beeping. The little lieutenant stopped passing the wand and held it where the noise was seemed to originate from. She stopped it at his crotch, then moved it away, whereupon the beeping stopped. She looked at him suspiciously and moved the wand toward and away from his crotch again. Each time the wand beeped loudly when it was near his crotch and stopped when it was moved away from his crotch.

A few in the crowd on line started to applaud. "The brother is bionic. He don't got a wood rod, he got a real rod," said a male voice from the line.

"Alright, dude. What you got in there?" asked the surly lieutenant as a two male security officers started to slowly work their way to his area.

"It ain't *that* kind of weapon," said Dexter and reflexively grabbed his genitals, whereupon he immediately realized the problem. A small coin had wedged itself in the creased corner of his front pocket to the right his pants zipper. He reached in the pocket and fumbled a few times attempting to pull the coin out, before finally pulling it out and handing it to the lieutenant.

She wanded him again, but this time there was no beeping.

"Guess you're gonna have to undress somebody else," said Dexter and walked to the table that had his belongings in a tray.

HE COULD OVERHEAR THE heated exchange of voices coming from the conference room a few doors away from where he was sitting. The volume of one of the voices was beginning to rise and he could hear other voices in the room, besides the two main voices.

Without warning, the conference room door flew open and a well-dressed man in a dark business suit walked to the receptionist and reached for her phone. During the opening and closing of the door, Dexter could hear that the heated exchanges were still going on. The man in the dark suit dialed a number and waited.

"Hello, Sam. This is Harold Goldstein. I told you earlier that I didn't have any officers here for conferences and you promised to send me two. I've got an uncooperative, belligerent individual up here who is getting out of hand. I need you to get up off your slow ass and send two of your biggest officers up here to the conference room immediately; this is getting ugly and I want this gentleman to be restrained and/or detained!" He abruptly slammed the phone down and stormed back to the conference room. As he opened the door, more heated exchanges escaped from the room.

Fifteen minutes later the receptionist said, "Mr. Reed, Mr. Goldstein will have you come into the Hearing Room now." He never saw anyone come out, or any officers go in. There must be another entry he thought.

Dexter entered a medium sized conference room with a fifteen-foot long table in the middle of the room. It had six chairs on either side length wise and one at each end. On one side four men in dark business suits sat side-by-side with papers spread in front of each of them. One of them got up upon Dexter's entry with the receptionist, and introduced himself.

"Good morning, Mr. Reed. My name is Harold Goldstein. I am the Assistant Director to the Inspector General of New York City," he said, and introduced the other men at the table, then asked Dexter to have a seat. Dexter realized that these were attempts at intimidation tactics, however, they were somewhat effective.

"First, for the record, what is your name?"

"My name is Dexter Reed."

"Where do you work Mr. Reed?"

"I work for the South Bronx Ambulance Company."

"What is your title at the South Bronx Ambulance Company?"

"I am an Emergency Medical Technician."

"So part of your job is to respond to 9-1-1 ambulance calls for medical emergencies?"

"Yes."

"How long have you worked for the South Bronx Ambulance Company, Mr. Reed?"

"I have worked for them for the past two and a half years."

"Mr. Reed, this is a preliminary investigative hearing and it is being recorded by our court stenographer, Mrs. Edwards, at the end of the table. You have been requested to appear because of apparent activities that are violations of the New York City Code regarding Section 31. It carries a possible penalty of 5-7 years in prison and a five thousand dollar fine."

More intimidation thought Dexter. When are they going to get to the guts of this?

"Over the past nine months, Mr. Reed, while working for the South Bronx Ambulance Company, you have transported approximately thirty-five patients to the hospital that became clients of one particular Bronx law firm. That is highly irregular."

"We are offering you a chance to cooperate with this investigation and help us catch the bigger fish, the attorneys and doctors who are ripping off the public for hundreds of thousands, if not millions, of dollars. If you cooperate, you would receive a slap on the wrist at most, compared to the possibility of losing your New York State EMT certification, a fine and jail. " There was a pause, waiting for Dexter to respond.

"Mr. Goldstein, I have no business connection with any attorneys or doctors at all, whether in the Bronx, or the state, or the country."

"We have proof that your partner was involved in these illicit activities. What we are trying to determine is if you were: an unknowing, unaware participant; or whether you had knowledge of the activities but failed to properly notify your boss or the authorities; or whether you were an active accomplice receiving monetary gain for your involvement."

"Mr. Goldstein, I have come here to show my desire to cooperate with your investigation. However, as I said, I have no connection to any attorney or doctor, and I have no control over my partner or any alleged illicit activity on his part..."

One of the suits sitting at the table seemed irritated, he interrupted, "Mr. Reed, what we have here is a case of an ambulance chaser with illegal immediate access to injured patients, who then sends his clients to collusive doctor's offices. It would appear that you are not cooperating fully, and therefore impeding this investigation. Are you aware of the consequences of the impeding these investigations?"

"I don't remember your name sir, but with all due respect, what we have here so far is a case of allegation and speculation. I don't know what evidence you have against me, beside the circumstantial evidence offered in an irregular statistic, but I am beginning to feel like a murder suspect being interrogated by the District Attorney."

"If you have evidence that I did something wrong, then please present it. If not, then I am going to leave and we can schedule another hearing where I will bring legal counsel," said Dexter as he rose from his chair.

That was really ballsy, thought Dexter. Now what do you do? Walk out and get detained at the door? Maybe the situation called for a dramatic display.

"Sit down, Mr. Reed," demanded Goldstein, surprised and frustrated with yet another loss of emotional control by an individual being questioned.

Dexter glared at Goldstein angrily.

"I said, sit down Mr. Reed!"

"I don't know who you think you are talking to, but this session is over," said Dexter as he began to walk away from the table.

"Wait, Mr. Reed. I'm sorry, things are a little tense in here from the last hearing. *Please* sit down," said Goldstein, with an emphasis on the please.

Dexter looked Goldstein in the eye searching for sincerity and was satisfied. He sat down.

"We are going through a period of gathering information and facts, then discerning the verity and validity of said information and facts, before we make a prosecution decision. It would help us, and you, if we had a clearer idea of the facts. And as I alluded to earlier, we are after the big players in this, the corrupt doctors, lawyers and others that have engaged in illegal activities that cost taxpayers and insurance companies what could be millions of dollars."

Dexter stuck to his guns and denied any knowledge or participation with any law firms in the Bronx. He left the Inspector General's office feeling they believed him, although he still wanted to kick Goldstein's ass.

CHAPTER

11

    RICO SAT AT HIS DESK at the Spellman Law Offices. The floor-to-ceiling wood paneling seemed dull and lackluster in the modest sized office. His desk was isolated in a back corner. His stock portfolio had taken a hit recently, and Rico pondered cashing in his chips. His gut told him to withdraw all his money from the stock market and re-invest it elsewhere, or put it in hiding for a little while.

    Happenings over the past few days had given Rico cause to pause. First, Eve was starting to show signs of possessiveness, jealousy and insecurity. She began to clock him, wanting to know why he didn't or couldn't come by her apartment on a given night. Why was he late? She would tell him how many hours or days they were together this week and compare the totals of hours or days to last week's or last month's, and point out a drastic drop off. She had begun to accuse him of having other women, which led to arguing. The arguing caused him to avoid her somewhat, and affected the frequency of sex. The intensity and passion was there during sex, she was still a gorgeous piece of ass in his eyes, but the magic of 'love' had worn off and she was no longer Pocahontas, his ravishing Taino Indian beauty. He had discovered grave imperfections in his Mona Lisa.

To make matters worse, one night he had come out the bathroom and found her going through his cell phone messages and numbers. She was irate that he was still in contact with an ex-girlfriend and that the ex was still texting him. Rico wasn't fucking her, so he didn't see the harm. But an argument ensued and Eve became Evil-lyn. Rico put on his clothes and headed for the door, but she wasn't finished. She stepped in front of Rico and blocked the apartment exit door while screaming at him about fucking the ex. Rico shoved her, causing her to stumble and fall to the tiled floor; she used her hands to break her fall. He later found out that she fractured her wrist. His anger over her invasion of his privacy later turned to remorse and shame. He had never struck a woman before and was strongly against beating women. Guys bragged about it in jail, but he kept his feelings quiet. He always felt it was better to walk away from the heat of the moment, or the relationship. Besides, the last thing he needed was to be arrested for a simple Domestic Violence rap. He had been in makeup mode since then, and although still angry, Eve began enjoying the attention and gifts.

Next, Spellman was showing signs of an about-face. For a while he had become less rigid in their relationship, almost friendly, but lately appeared constantly tense and irritable. His words were biting and full of sarcasm. Rico wondered if it was due to the economic recession and its effect on the stock market and his portfolio, or the fact that case settlements had slowed down at the firm. In a few minutes he would go into Spellman's office to give his updates on pending cases and let Spellman know the bad news on the 'kid out the window' case.

Finally, Rico had received word from Roman Reyes about the IG's investigation into the connection between ambulance calls and Spellman's law firm. Spellman would probably explode behind the news.

DEXTER SAT ON A BRONX park bench watching dozens of small kids run back and forth on the gated playground under the overcast sky. The rubberized mats on the ground prevented fall injuries and added a soft plodding sound to their steps, while also muting their screams of laughter.

Roman broke away from a group of kids, leaving them with his wife, and walked over to Dexter. Dexter stood up and gave the South Bronx handshake to Roman while they gave each other a half embrace. Roman's three-year-old autistic son broke away from the mother and the others, and ran over to Roman. Dexter smiled, "Hey RayRay. High five, low five, fist bump and a hug." RayRay smiled and did their usual greeting routine, following Dexter's lead. He picked the boy up and held him high over his head, as RayRay squealed gleefully. Dexter put RayRay down and looked up to see Maria smiling and waving from across the play area. He smiled and waved back, tapping his heart twice. She tapped hers back.

Although normal in appearance, RayRay didn't communicate verbally, only making indistinguishable sounds and an occasional word. He had normal coordination and kept up with the other kids physically, but where the other three year olds talked in short sentences, RayRay could only cry, whine or laugh. Roman confided that it tore at Roman's heart to see his son suffer through this, but he put up a gallant front for others. The specialists told Roman and Maria that with therapy RayRay might be able to lead a normal, productive life.

"So what's the word?" asked Dexter.

"From what they are saying, they had an insider watching me and clocking me on the scene of some of the accident calls. Their snitch observed me making cell phone calls at the scene," said Roman.

They looked at each other, shook their heads and at the same time said, "...fucking Newby".

"That means, Newby was a cheese-eater and a plant from the beginning," said Dexter. "No wonder he didn't show up to work after all the IG letters started flowing."

"Yep. Something inside told me not to trust that Big Bird looking muthafucka. But, luckily Rico, my contact at the law firm, kept me in steady supply of disposable cell phones. Their whole case is built on Newby and circumstantial evidence. What are they doing in your case?"

"My case? They don't have anything on me. They're threatening me with being an 'Accessory During the Fact', and trying to pressure me into giving them info on you, which I won't do, and which frustrates the hell out of them," said Dexter.

"Cool. I'm trying to get Rico to get his people to hire a lawyer for me, but I'm getting double talk from him. They can't represent me because it gives the appearance that we are working together, and hiring an outside law firm could cost them six figures. The City has a reputation for drawing these things out for five, six, seven years, if they don't like the verdict."

"Yeah, at the taxpayer's expense," acknowledged Dexter, while tugging on RayRay's cap as he sat at their feet playing with a toy plastic dinosaur.

"Yo, Dex, I'm considering bluffing 'em and telling 'em I'm thinking about taking a plea bargain if they don't get me a lawyer. Spook 'em. You know, act like I'm really worried and ready to sing about everything just to see what they do, 'cause I gotta get this thing over. "

"Yeah, this suspension sucks and it's probably part of their strategy, figuring we'll talk like a parrot after missing a couple of paychecks. I've killed my reserves already. The only good thing from this is that I've had extra time to crack the books and stay on top of the paramedic course. Tomorrow I have to make a few calls and find out if we get our back pay when this is resolved, without charges. Also, whether the state is going to temporarily suspend our EMT certifications and start looking up our asses. We would be totally screwed if the state decided to take away our livelihood behind this bullshit," said Dexter. "We could take a big hit behind this. I might not be allowed to take my New York State paramedic exam. All that money and time could get flushed down the toilet...plus lose my EMT certification, job and have to work McDonald's."

"My girl is squeezing me to quit working and move in with her 'temporarily'. I wasn't feeling that before, but now it's a strong possibility, since I don't have an income. I'm late with my rent and my credit card, so far. Man, I warned you when you first spoke to me about this hook up with the attorney's office that this could lead to big problems. Now look at where this bullshit has taken us. I'm suspended from work, no paycheck, about to get kicked out of my apartment, my girlfriend pressuring me to move in with her, and the state may take away my license and not let me take the paramedic exam. All this and I never took a dime! "

"Dex, I am truly sorry you got dragged into this shit, bro. This was supposed to be just another hustle, a way for me to make a few extra bucks, off the books, that the ex and the courts couldn't touch. I can't wait for this shit to be over. As a matter of fact, I'm gonna call Rico on the disposable phone now and tell him we need to talk 'cause I'm feeling a song in my throat. Then, I'm gonna drive up and down Long Island until I find that punkass bitch, Newby."

"Yeah, I gotta make a call myself. One of my boys left a message that his agent is interested in me and wants to talk about signing a contract with him. He says his agent is promising to get me on a pro-team in the new ABA League," said Dexter. "Imagine that, getting paid to play ball."

"Really?"

"Yeah. But it's not NBA money. I think most of the players have 9-5 jobs and play their games on the weekends. They get about three hundred a week, fed and a charter bus to away games, mainly on the East Coast, like Philly, DC and Baltimore."

RICO WAS GATHERING his case files in preparation for his weekly case conference with Spellman, when the throwaway phone rang. "Whazup?"

"Yo, Rico, we gotta talk soon. I'm getting squeezed by the IG's office, man. They're sweating me big time and threatening me with serious jail time, if I don't cooperate and give them names, places and dates to someone in the law firm. Listen, your guys gotta get me a lawyer, man. Meanwhile, throughout all this I haven't got paid for nearly three weeks. I feel like I'm being left to hang out to dry, while you guys are drinking champagne and eating caviar. I'm hurtin' bad, man. Throw me a life raft, brother."

"Alright. I was on my way into the boss' office in a minute. I'll see what I can do. Where are you?"

"I'm in the park with my kids. Get back to me as soon as you can," said Roman and then hung up. "Was I convincing? Did I sound desperate enough," said Roman smiling at Dexter.

"YES, OF COURSE I have advised my client of your offer! And after our consultation he decided to reject your company's offer. You have the hubris and temerity to question my knowledge of the law, sir? Or are you questioning my ethics? Your question sounds like you are either inferring that I am incompetent or unethical or both."

Spellman paused as the opposing party's insurance rep stumbled with some form of apology. "I've probably been practicing law longer than you've been on the earth. But let me be clear, we have been very patient with your company, but apparently to no avail. It would seem that court papers should be filed and a court date should be scheduled. If we don't hear a reasonable and substantial improvement in your offer in one week, then we shall proceed with filing for a docket number. Good day, sir," said Spellman, then abruptly hung up the phone.

Rico couldn't tell if Spellman was truly upset or whether it was another performance. But whether heated or performing, he still looked quite dapper in his custom made, monogrammed, white dress shirt and solid fuchsia tie, sitting behind his large oak desk. The brightness from the white shirt was a perfect contrast to his smooth tanned skin.

"Carmen, hold all calls for about twenty minutes. Rico and I are in conference in my office," said Spellman into his desk phone.

"All right Rico, give me the updates on the pending files. I need some good news for a change."

"The Angel Rivera case is a no-go. New York Case Law and New York Statutes are against us on a few grounds. First, while the window-guard laws require landlords to provide window guards in apartments where children 10 years of age or under reside, a landlord is not liable for falls from unguarded windows unless the child is a resident of the apartment unit. In our case, the little girl was only two years old, but her mother was not on the lease. They only lived in the apartment for three months and the lessee was not a blood relative, only a friend. Further, my sources say the mother is a crack-head and on the night of accident left the little girl alone for a short period of time to purchase drugs."

Spellman nodded as he wrote some notes on a legal pad, as was his usual custom. He would make a copy and give it to Rico with instructions on it. Rico went over six more files - saving the IG for last, due to his involvement, the complications of the case, and its criticalness.

Rico put the pile of files on the floor next to him and sat back in his chair looking Spellman in his eyes. "Lastly, a critical situation has developed that is not one of the files. It involves my recruitment of cases for the firm, and more specifically, the government's questioning of one of my paid informants."

"Yes, I know about the Office of the Inspector General's investigation into a connection between this law firm and certain personal injury lawsuits. What else do I need to know?" said Spellman.

Rico was surprised but continued… "One of my ambulance informants was set up with a government plant working on his ambulance. Now the IG is questioning my ambulance informant and trying to intimidate him into giving up information to implicate this law firm. My guy says he is worried about jail time and needs legal representation. Without a lawyer he might take a plea and give the firm up."

Spellman's face was cold and impassionate. They sat there in silence for a moment. No movement of facial muscles, his eyes just staring straight at and through Rico, but Rico knew his mind was moving at light-speed and was developing a multi-layered plan.

"Call this guy up on one of the disposable phones I gave you and set up a meeting. Tomorrow. At a public -but secluded spot in New Jersey, something just over the bridge not far away. Let me know right away as soon as you know when and where. I will go with you and meet him, but don't tell him I'm coming. Tell him you're bringing a lawyer," said Spellman finally.

"How does Franco's Restaurant in Fort Lee at 7pm sound?"

"Perfect," said Spellman.

DEXTER LOOKED AT the caller ID on his ringing cell phone and answered, "Hey, Romie. What's up?"

"Guess what just happened."

"I don't know. Either the Dominican says she's pregnant with twins, or you found out you got a STD?"

"Nah college boy, get serious. Rico just called me. My plan worked. He wants to meet me at a restaurant just over the bridge in Jersey tomorrow and he's bringing a lawyer to discuss legal strategy," said Roman.

"Cool. Check this out, Bob Brogan just called me. He says he just got official word that the IG dropped my part of the investigation and I can go back to work tomorrow."

"It's about damn time. Now, hopefully Rico's lawyers can get the same results for me. Did you find out from the union if we can get our back pay for this?"

"No, they haven't gotten back to me yet."

"Yeah, but they can snatch our dues in a heartbeat, right?" snorted Roman.

"I know the Vice President of the Local. I'll call him direct tomorrow, he's good people."

RICO ARRIVED AT THE restaurant thirty minutes early to case the layout, so he could determine the best and worst tables. He entered Franco's and glanced around. Sitting next to the entry door or the bathroom was a pet-peeve of his and was to be avoided at all costs. Maybe that was a lingering effect from prison. A huge bar that extended from one side of the moderately lit restaurant to the other side, and forced arriving patrons to go left or right, blocked his path. The headwaiter greeted him and asked how many in the party, then lead Rico around the long bar toward the dining area and tables. Rico stopped abruptly. Over in a quiet secluded corner was Spellman! Rico hadn't noticed any of Spellman's cars in the parking lot. Wise and crafty, thought Rico. Maybe he parked around the corner in case the IG was tailing Roman. That's probably why he called Rico and told him he would meet them in New Jersey.

Rico panned the restaurant for the other customers. It was the middle of the week and it was about 1/4 full. There were couples and small families spread throughout the restaurant, but a gentleman reading the Wall Street Journal sitting alone caught Rico's attention. He seemed out of place. His clean-shaven, crew cut appearance and bland dark gray suit with an open collared white shirt, seemed more suited for government or military business. The gentleman had a strange two-inch scar near his right temple area that looked like an old burn wound. Rico shrugged it off, probably waiting for his wife or mistress to come out the bathroom he thought, and walked over to Spellman.

Spellman was all business, dressed in a dark blue suit with pinstripes, white shirt and a powder blue tie and breast pocket kerchief. While sipping a cup of coffee with one hand he gestured for Rico to have a seat next to him with the other hand. "We have to go over a few things; ground rules you might say. First, don't give your informant my name, simply state that I am an attorney. Second, after introductions and pleasantries are exchanged let me direct the flow of the questions and direction of the conversation. I need to fully assess where this guy's head is, and if he is a threat. You have disappointed me with your selection of him as a resource. He is weak, shaky and undisciplined."

"Finally, this is going to be no more than a twenty minute affair. I have another meeting I have to attend after this one. You can stay with him if you want, but I advise you to leave shortly after me," said Spellman between sips.

Rico nodded, but his mind was caught on Spellman's tone, almost like a reprimand or verbal spanking. He had been fighting the urge lately, but was even more so tempted to tell Spellman to kiss his ass.

"You know, your attitude toward me lately has become pretty shitty. We are approaching a point where I am just about fed up with your obnoxious ass, STEVE. The fact that you sign my paycheck doesn't make me your whore or your slave, and I am not going to shine your shoes or kiss your ass."

Spellman put his coffee down and looked at Rico sternly. "I know everything about you, son. Do you think I would hire you and not do a background check on you? Do you think that I wouldn't find out about your criminal background or your activity with legal research while in prison? Do you think I would give you all this money and not monitor your activities? A man in my position has to be aware of everything. I make enough money to know who in my office is earning their pay and who isn't, who is bad-mouthing me and who isn't, who is stealing from me and who isn't! I have known about your set up with your informants and I've monitored it with interest, amusement and a little trepidation. I hired you and gave you a second chance. When I found out that you were a motivated, strong willed person, I rewarded you. But I monitored you, just like I monitor everyone in my office, even my attorney wife. I spent a lot of money on a security system that enables me to know what's being said in each office and on each phone. I even bought disposable phones and placed bugs and tracking devices in them. I know who you and your resources talk to and can trace your movements, if necessary. I know everything, like the fact that you are considering terminating your employment with my office without discussing it or asking my permission. I know about you and my wife. You have failed me and disappointed me, and I told you once I don't tolerate failure...," Spellman stopped short as Roman walked toward their table.

Rico was about to explode on Spellman. He wanted so badly to plant a right hand cross on Spellman's jaw but composed himself, stood up and extended his hand to Roman, "Hi Roman, how are you doing? Glad you could make it. Have a seat. This is an attorney I brought along to hear what's going on with the IG's investigation and advise us where to go from here. "

Roman sat and nodded toward Spellman, "Good Rico, 'cause like I told you, they are squeezing me big time with threats of prison, and I feel like I'm on an island by myself with no help from you guys."

Spellman coolly and calmly stepped into the conversation and asked Roman, "What do they know so far, with regard to you and the law firm? And what evidence have they presented against you?"

"Nothing. They know nothing and they have presented nothing. They are going by the amount of cases that I responded to on the ambulance that wound up being represented by Rico's firm. The only real evidence they've presented has been a plant they placed on the ambulance, as a bogus employee. This plant claims, he saw me on the phone making calls from the scene of accidents. That's it. But they wanna throw me in jail for not helping them and not giving up the big players. It seems that my testimony is vital to them and vital for Rico's law firm. It all hinges on me and what I say."

"So tell us Roman, what do you want, or need, from 'Rico's law firm' to resolve this?" asked Spellman.

"I'm glad you asked. I told Rico, I need an attorney to represent me in these hearings. What I didn't tell Rico is that I also need cash. I haven't gotten paid from my job for nearly three weeks while these investigations and hearings are going on. So 'what I need' is an attorney AND about ten grand cash, to keep quiet. And I need it in forty-eight hours, or I start singing. I ain't gonna go to jail for you guys."

Rico tried hard to keep the astonishment and shock from registering on his face. This was turning ugly, he thought. Roman was turning greedy, going from 'he needed an attorney' to demanding blackmail money. Rico didn't expect this from Roman and never saw it coming. Rico looked to Spellman's reaction, and just then he saw him make eye contact with the government looking guy in the gray suit and nod, then they looked quickly away from each. The gray suit got up from his table, grabbed his long coat and bill, then walked toward the front of the restaurant.

"Okay, Roman. I will have to take your demands to my bosses for approval. Rico will be in contact with you soon," said Spellman. "Do you have any other requests or problems that need to be addressed?"

Roman shook his head. "I mean I do have two ex-wives that are problems, but the pressing problems right now are these two items," trying to interject some humor into the situation, but Spellman wasn't smiling.

"Well then, I must leave and relay this information to my superiors immediately. They insist on getting news promptly, especially bad news. He got up straight-faced from the table, shook hands, grabbed his coat and walked toward the front of the restaurant.

Rico sat in his chair, shaking his head, looking at Roman. "What the fuck did you just do?"

"Sorry, Rico, but I had to speed up the process. You and your people were doing a turtle dance."

"You just painted a big red target on our backs with blood, and the shark is circling."

"Fuck that, I told you I ain't going to jail for you guys. Unlike you, I got a wife and kids to feed. So somebody better come up with a lawyer and some cash, quick."

Rico sat back at the restaurant table thinking he either needed a cigarette or a stiff drink. Maybe both.

CHAPTER

12

ROMAN STRODE CONFIDENTLY to his minivan in the restaurant parking lot. He felt elated about the meeting that had just transpired and was confident that the lawyer believed he was desperate, and ready to sing. He was so ecstatic over the potential to get money that he wasn't aware of the man stepping from the shadows, as he pressed the automatic unlock for his car door. He never heard the chirp-chirp as the shadowy figure hit him over the head with a leather covered blackjack. The shadowy figure grabbed Roman under his armpits before he hit the ground and opened the back door with his free hand. He pushed Roman into the back of the minivan face down on the floor, closed the door, then picked up the keys off the ground.

He drove six blocks east from the restaurant, passed a group of abandoned buildings that he had cased earlier in the day to ensure there were no cameras. He parked, reached back and took Roman's watch, ring, necklace and wallet, then jumped into the back seat from the driver's seat. He turned Roman over to check for any personal papers in his pockets when Roman suddenly stirred. The shadowy figure pulled out a hand gun with a silencer on it and shot Roman three times in the chest, center mass, at point blank range. He was aiming to hit a chamber of the heart with each bullet. Roman's body slumped down and the shooter watched as Roman took his last breath. He finished checking for personal papers then got out the minivan and closed the door. As he walked back to where he had parked his car near the restaurant, he checked his leather gloves and clothing for any blood splatter.

DEXTER AND HIS NEW PARTNER, Sandra Berry, got out of the ambulance and walked toward the body on the pavement in front of the grocery store entrance. One man stood over him while people entered and left the store on their way to work in the early AM, pausing momentarily to look down at the person on the ground. He looked at the owner of the store and asked, "What happened?" He knelt down and felt for a carotid pulse in the neck with his latex gloved hand.

"Somebody came inside the store and said there was a man outside having a seizure on the ground. When I got outside, I found him laying there like this and I called 9-1-1," said the little balding man.

"Pedro. Pedro. Are you okay?" said Dexter loudly as he shook the man's shoulder again and timed his breathing by the rise and fall of his chest. He probably was sitting outside the grocery store all night and now it's time to clear him out before he frightens away the morning crowd, thought Dexter.

"He's lying on the cold concrete, barely conscious and you're asking him if he's okay? What the hell do you think, man?" spoke one of a group of three teenage patrons exiting the grocery store in a sarcastic and challenging tone.

"Yeah, you ain't nothing but a stretcher-fetcher. Pick his ass up, put him on the stretcher and take him to the hospital," chided another teenager.

"Took you forever to get here, he coulda been dead by now," chimed in another. The teens glared at Dexter and the scene over their shoulders as they walked toward the subway, dropping their feigned community anger and laughingly fist bumping each other.

Dexter was accustomed to the extreme remarks that New York City bystanders, patients and patient's family or friends occasionally hurled at first responders. It was part of any job that required dealing with the public; the criticisms were hurled often while the praise, thanks and appreciation were rarely seen or heard. Dexter continued his assessment of the patient without missing a beat, trying to get a response and gauge his mental alertness. "This is Pedro, one of the neighborhood alcohol abusers. I'm surprised you don't know him at your store." The storeowner shrugged indifference, merely wanting to have the human obstruction removed from the front of his store.

Pedro stirred, then growled at Dexter with slurred speech, as he pushed Dexter's hand away from his shoulder. The smells of alcohol, from his breath, and urine, from his clothes, combined to make an all too familiar pungent stench to Dexter. Pedro was one of the regulars in the area. A 'frequent flyer' as Roman would call him. When almost sober, Pedro would extol with pride his career as a professional boxer in his youth. Dexter, during calls with Pedro as a patient, would tease him that he couldn't have been a good boxer, because he had a glass jaw and it seemed that the Rum hit him every day.

"Leave me alone. Get off me," growled Pedro, again pushing Dexter's gloved hand off his shoulder.

"It's EMS, Pedro. You've had a seizure. We're here to help you and take you to the hospital."

Pedro stopped shoving Dexter's hand and squinted, trying to focus on his face. "Yeah, EMS, I know you. You the one that don't know shit about boxin'. I could probably kick your ass right now. You tall like Mendez was, but I knocked Mendez out. Mendez had no heart. All he wanted to do was jab and run. You got heart, EMS? Wanna go a few rounds with old Pedro?" and he attempted to get to his feet. Sandra Berry had gotten the ambulance stair chair opened and positioned it behind Pedro. He stumbled getting up but Dexter caught him under one arm and a NYPD officer, just arriving on the scene, caught him under the other arm. They gently guided him into the wheel-chair, then took him to the ambulance, lifted him in and transported him to the hospital. Dexter thanked the cop for his assistance. He stayed in the back with Pedro and had Sandra drive, out of concern that Pedro might try to grope and grab her, and not sure what her response might be, since they hadn't worked together often. He had the feeling that she might try to knock Pedro's head off if he grabbed her butt or a breast.

During the ride to the hospital, Dexter remembered that two weeks ago he took Pedro to the hospital under similar conditions with Roman riding in the back with Pedro. They chummed it up. Roman had Pedro laughing almost non-stop during the ride. Afterward, Roman remarked about all of the scars covering Pedro's eyes and face, and a nose that had an "S" curve in it.

Dexter observed the scars now, as Pedro lay face up on the stretcher, wondering how much of it came from boxing and how much of it came from a post-boxing life-style of poverty, depression and excessive drinking. Dexter began to be reacquainted with the overpowering odor of urine coming from Pedro, while they traveled in the closed patient compartment in the back of the ambulance. He had neglected to open the window or turn on the vent fan; now his sense of smell was under full-fledged attack. He quickly reached over to the control panel on the wall and activated the power vent fan. He heard the motor kick on and the fan start up. Now the challenge was, could he hold his breath for two minutes until the odor was removed, he thought.

"Hey, EMS. Where's the other guy, the Puerto Rican guy?"

"I don't know, haven't seen him for a while. But Pedro it's 6:30 in the morning, what's going on? Is this leftover from yesterday or are you getting a head start on today?"

It wasn't like Romie to not answer Dexter's calls. The most was a day later. But he hadn't heard from him in a few days which seemed unusual, even with Romie chasing after Dominican panties. Calling his wife wasn't a good idea either, thought Dexter. If he hadn't been home recently she would either be angrily cursing him out, or crying inconsolably out of worry.

As he and Sandra sat in the hospital EMS room after the call, Dexter started some small talk to open lines of communications, since it looked like they were going to be partners until Roman came back.

"Hey Sandra, you got any kids?"

"Yeah, I have two girls. They are the loves of my life. Why?" she asked suspiciously.

"Easy, girl. Just wondering. It looks like we are going to be working together for a while, I thought we should get to know each other a little better."

"Better like how? There's really nothing to know about me. I'm Jewish, a mother of two, and going to nursing school."

"That's fine for starters, I'm not looking for your life story. I'll wait for the book and the movie," smiled Dexter.

She smiled for what seemed like the first time that he could recall.

"Married?"

"No, going through a nasty divorce with an asshole of a guy. He refuses to pay anything for his daughters, and I have to drag him into court to make him financially support his own flesh and blood. His parents are rich and get him the best lawyers against me then, on our court date, he doesn't show up after I've taken the day off from work to appear. I work midnights now, so that I don't have to miss days when I go to court, and also so I can be home for my kids in the day."

"So the wedding ring is to ward off the wolves?"

"Yeah," she chuckled. "But I don't know if it really works. The wolves are oblivious to it, or they just don't care. I'm at the point where I hate men. They all seem to have a one-track mind. Your boy Roman, is a prime example. My focus is all about raising my girls. What about you?"

"As you know, I've been working here for a few years as an EMT, while taking paramedic classes. I've been going out with this nice woman for a while and I'm totally satisfied with her. No marriage or kids on the horizon."

"Good for you. You seem like one of the nice guys around here. I like the way you talk to the patients and their family, very respectfully and professionally. I noticed how you handled the drunk guy just now, and you were considerate and gentlemanly enough to take over patient care, so that I could drive and not be in the back of the ambulance alone with him. Thank you."

"I'm glad we're working together. Some of these guys at the job are a trip. One guy was trying to pick up girls by talking to them over the loudspeaker/PA system on the ambulance. How crude and unprofessional can they be? And does that stuff work? Do women go for that approach? I guess so, if the guys continually do it. Even if it only worked once there's a chance it could work again, I guess," she reasoned.

"Don't judge all by the few. There are a lot of good people in EMS. It's just unfortunate that bad decisions by the few, at bad times, make it to the front page of the media and give the whole EMS community a black eye," said Dexter. He had gotten her to open up, now he couldn't shut her off, he thought. He found out that she was a very bright woman, well read and versed on many subjects. She made her daughters the center of her universe. Her life consisted of family, work and school. No time for partying, socializing or men. An only child, she married young and divorced young, without many friends and without much social experience, especially with men. Her rigidity toward men was her primary defense, balanced with a sharp intellect that intimidated many men and an obsessive-compulsive disorder to cleanliness. She wouldn't allow guys to touch her, let alone kiss her, unless she felt they were clean. She masked and gloved up at the beginning of every call.

She was a good partner to have on the ambulance because she cleaned everything, made sure the equipment worked and was in its proper place. A big difference from Roman, Dexter thought.

After leaving the hospital and driving back to their area, with Sandra going on in great detail about the awards her daughters were winning academically and artistically, Dexter noticed a man run into the street about fifty feet in front of the ambulance. The young black male was waving frantically, the headlights from the ambulance shone like a spotlight on his dark skin, black jeans and navy blue tee shirt with the USA Olympic basketball logo on its front. "Yo, EMS. Stop, Stop!"

Dexter stopped the ambulance and got out of the driver's side. He started to walk over to the man, who ran over to him and panted, "Listen, someone shot my man. He's in the hall, come help him."

Dexter reached back into the ambulance, grabbed the radio microphone and transmitted, "Central, be advised, SoBro One had been flagged down for a possible shooting in the hallway of 5555 Bergen Ave. Please have PD respond."

"Come on man, you gotta hurry up. He's shot."

Dexter put the microphone down on the console and looked over at Sandra, who hadn't moved from her seat in the ambulance the whole time. "Dexter, protocols say we should wait for PD to arrive and the scene is safe. The shooter could still be in there."

The young man who flagged them down was standing next to Dexter and heard Sandra's remarks. "Wait for shit. My man is laying on the ground in there bleeding to death, do your job, give him medical attention, get him to the hospital."

Dexter understood Sandra's reservation, she was right. The shooter or shooters could still be in there, and she had her daughters she needed to go home to at the end of her shift. It wasn't worth the risk of possibly losing her life. But Dexter couldn't sit by and wait for the police to arrive... a life was at stake and every second was vitally important. What if it were his brother, or what if were him in there? Besides, Dexter reasoned, this was the ghetto, no one shoots another person and hangs around for the cops, news reporters and camera crews. The shooter, more than likely, became an Olympic track star right after the shooting and was gone before the echo of the shots had died. He was probably in another borough or another state by now, thought Dexter.

"Please, EMS. C'mon, do something, that's my man, he's like a brother to me."

Dexter walked to the back of the ambulance, pulled out the stretcher and grabbed equipment, quickly throwing it on to the stretcher. "Let's go," he said, pushing the stretcher toward the ten-story NYC Housing Projects building entrance, in a slight jog behind the victim's friend.

As they entered the building there was a long, well lit lobby with a three elevator bank at the end. The building was unusually clean, thought Dexter as he observed everything, trying to be aware of suspicious characters slithering in the background. They hurried past a wall full of mailboxes. One of the elevator doors was open, held open by the body on the ground half in the elevator and half out.

Dexter ran over to the body and checked for a pulse. The victim still had a faint, thready pulse and lay there in a pool of blood around his torso. Dexter cut open the shirt to find three bullet wounds in the chest. One of the wounds was a sucking chest wound that he bandaged right away. While bandaging the chest wound he heard footsteps approaching him and voices transmitting on radio frequencies. He looked up to see Sandra walking quickly toward him with an oxygen bag and a spinal immobilization board.

NYPD arrived moments later, as Dexter and Sandra put the patient on the stretcher. They wheeled the stretcher with the immobilized, bandaged patient on oxygen, and carried him out of the lobby. A paramedic unit, a Fire Department basic EMS unit and a Fire Department EMS Lieutenant rushed over to assist them.

The EMS Lieutenant called in a 'notification' while they were enroute to the hospital and the trauma team was prepped and ready as soon as they arrived at the Emergency Department doors. Dexter helped wheel the stretcher into the largest of the trauma rooms, as the team of twelve hospital personnel started moving to do their individual duties.

The lead doctor, in hospital scrubs, gloves, mask and head cap started asking the medics questions while listening to lung sounds, and the nurse checked the intravenous line, took vital signs and started cutting off all clothes and removing jewelry from the patient. Another doctor was prepping a surgical kit, preparing to crack the patient's chest open, while an anesthesiologist checked the endotracheal tube in the patient's throat and began attaching a breathing apparatus to it. Another nurse was rolling a tray with more bags of IV's, trauma dressings and other equipment on it to the side of the stretcher. A clerical staff positioned themselves next to Dexter and added to the buzz in the room by asking, "Do you have any information on this patient so I can register him?"

"No, sorry Hilda. You're gonna have to John Doe him. We had to scoop and run with this guy, but he's got a buddy floating around here that claims to be like a brother, and should be able to give you some info. A brown skin guy wearing a blue Team USA t-shirt."

Dexter then peered over the crowd around the patient on the stretcher. The doctor on the side of the stretcher was making a horizontal incision along the front right chest of the young man on the stretcher. He then applied a surgical rib spreader into the incision, bracing it on the ribs above and below the incision, and began cranking it to create a space between them large enough to view and reach the patients lungs before they rushed him up to the Operating Room.

Dexter eased away from the beehive of buzzing activity in the trauma room, stepping over blood and discarded dressings on the beige tiled floor that was now smeared red, to go back to the ambulance and start his paperwork on the call.

At the opened back doors of the ambulance outside the hospital, he found Sandra inside, gloved, masked and wrapped toga style in a hospital sheet, wiping the ambulance benches, walls and cabinets down with cleansing agents.

"What happened back there?" he asked.

"I like you Dexter, I couldn't bear the idea of you getting shot and lying there bleeding to death, while I sat in the ambulance waiting for NYPD. Some of these other guys maybe, but not you. You're one of the good guys here."

He looked in her eyes and saw that she was sincere. But also saw something else. He sensed that quite possibly the frigid queen was smitten.

RICO SAT IN HIS car near his old 'Little Italy' neighborhood in the Bronx as the sun set on the horizon. He had parked on Southern Blvd near the Bronx Zoo smoking a cigarette while his mind raced a mile a minute. Who are the key players in this chess game, he wondered? Who could he trust? Who could he turn to for backup and support? Now, in retrospect, he was glad that he had put the Spellman off-the-books money in a safe untraceable investment. His initial concern was to avoid setting off any IRS red flags. Putting it somewhere that neither the feds nor Spellman would be able to trace, he invested it in the best 'bank' he knew. The bank his father and family swore by, and even though it wasn't federally insured, Rico felt it was safer than any commercial bank in the country.

Now he had to wisely figure out his next steps. This was going to be a chess match with Spellman, who he now realized was as ruthless as any of the inmates he knew in prison. Rico started to come up with the nucleus of a plan that began with setting up two safety nets. Being in his mid-twenties, the first safety net was going to be easy and inexpensive. The second safety net was going to involve a detailed explanation and a plan with someone he trusted. The only question was what kind of move would Spellman make, and when. Rico was a loose end for Spellman because Rico knew times, dates and details for all of the cases the authorities were interested in.   And with the dissension in the air, Spellman wouldn't risk gambling that Rico could talk and Spellman could possibly lose his lavish lifestyle for a cell, a cot, an orange jumpsuit and a cellmate named Bubba.

Spellman had mentioned in the restaurant that he knew about Rico and Michelle. Rico wondered if he knew the facts, or if he assumed that there was more. Rico had never touched her, outside of the momentary touching of hands in the office. Had Spellman tapped her phone and overheard her telling someone that she wanted to ride the young Italian stallion? She probably got whipped into a frenzy after seeing him in a swimming suit at poolside. Who knew Spellman was into tapping phones? Rico wondered if he listened to some of the conversations between Rico and Eve? She could be quite explicit in her requests of what she wanted. Was Spellman a pervert?

It was becoming increasingly clear to Rico that Spellman had too much to lose and that there was a high probability that Spellman was going to have a hit on him, like he had on Roman. He needed to mobilize his plans quickly. In the meantime, he had to figure out an immediate strategy for appearance purposes. Should he go to work tomorrow and act like he wasn't aware of Spellman's ruthlessness? Or should he lay low and avoid Spellman, which would probably make him more anxious. Rico's character wouldn't allow him to think at all about laying low and hiding from Spellman. Even if Spellman was waiting in his office with two cocked and loaded shotguns, Rico wouldn't run. That was never his style, even as a kid. When the older, bigger guys wanted to fight him after school, he would get there early and wait for them, prepped and ready to do battle. He saw it as a challenge; a test. There were no butterflies in his stomach, no anxiety. He thought back then that this is how a true warrior, gladiator or soldier must feel. The thrill and exhilaration of pending battle, no matter that the opponent was bigger, stronger, older, or, as was the case here with Spellman, with nearly unlimited resources.

Three young black guys had crossed the street, a few cars ahead of him. One was eyeing him in his car as they walked on the sidewalk in the direction of his car. The other two were engrossed in what appeared to be a friendly debate, while drinking beer from cans in paper bags. The one that was eyeballing stopped, bent over and lightly tapped on his front passenger window smilingly, as the other two continued walking and debating.

Rico's mind raced. Was this the hit? No, it couldn't be. It's too soon.

He watched as the other two kept walking, engrossed in their debate. Rico lowered the passenger window half way with the power button.

"Yo, man. Can you spare a cigarette? I forgot mine at home and none of these dudes smokes," asked the smiling young black man with a mouthful of crooked teeth.

"No problem cuz," said Rico. He handed him a nearly empty packet containing about three cigarettes through the half open window. Rico took a quick glance at his rear view mirror and checked that the other two hadn't doubled back. They hadn't stopped, although they'd slowed, they were still walking and debating. Smiley took one and handed the packet back. Rico shook his hand. "Keep 'em, brother."

"Thanks, man," said Smiley, then Rico saw the smile disappear from his face replaced with a stare at something over Rico's shoulder. He turned and noticed that a black Cadillac SUV with limousine-black tinted windows had pulled up next to him. He had been so concerned with Smiley and his crew that he wasn't aware of what was going on in the street. Smiley nodded to Rico then walked away, jogging to catch up with his buddies. As Rico watched him, it suddenly occurred to him that he didn't have a piece. It was a violation of parole for him to have any kind of weapon, but under these circumstances it would be suicide not to have a piece. He always liked the smaller Glocks, and made a mental note to get a clean one ASAP from one of his sources.

DEXTER WAS ON HIS WAY home from work after stopping to eat breakfast and get a newspaper, when his cell rang. The caller ID showed it was Roman's house. "Good fucking morning sunshine, where the hell you been?" barked Dexter.

A woman on the other end was sobbing and sniffling. "Dex, they found Roman dead...," followed by loud bawling.

"Maria is that you? What about Roman?"

It took a minute for Maria to gain her composure. "Dex, they found Roman dead in his car in New Jersey. The police think it was a robbery. They say he was shot three times and his watch, jewelry and wallet are gone. They came to me because of the New York registration and want me to come identify the body," then the emotional floodgates opened again.

"Okay, Maria. Stay at the apartment, I'll be there in ten minutes."

On the drive to Roman and Maria's apartment Dexter tried not to over react to what he had just heard. Denial, at first, had a strong grip, but now it was losing its strength. Roman dead? He and Romie were a team for only a few years, but those few EMS years were like fourteen in dog years. They did eight-hour shifts together five days a week regularly and extra shifts every other week. During those few years and thousands of shifts they got to know each other's innermost thoughts. Romie used to joke that they were married. Dexter felt more like they were brothers. He knew things about Romie that he didn't think his wives knew, current or ex-wives, his plans for his future, his career, his kids…

Dexter had to pull over. His body felt numb. No, it was his soul that was numb.

The noise from two dogs barking wildly at each other at the side of his car seemed to be coming from a city block away, far removed from his reality, while their young owners yelled at them in an attempt to ward off an imminent, spontaneous dog fight. Another small group of kids watched from the entry steps to a five-story apartment building with curious anticipation, hoping for some early morning excitement.

Dexter began putting the pieces of the puzzle together. Now it made sense why Romie hadn't returned his calls. It was obvious that the law firm was somehow involved in his apparent death. The last he had seen and spoken to Romie, he was excited about meeting his law firm contact, Rico, in *New Jersey* and excited that his *threat* had resulted in them capitulating into bringing a lawyer to the meeting. Romie had verbalized his intention to also squeeze them for money to make up for his and Dexter's lost pay. He probably 'over-spooked' them. Dexter wondered how much did Romie try to squeeze out of them?

Dexter wondered, would they come after him too? Would they consider him enough of a threat that they would want to kill him? Should he contact the IG's Office and tell them the truth about Romie and the law firm? Would the IG's Office want to prosecute him for lying initially? All these questions swirled in Dexter's head as he pulled off and drove up the Grand Concourse in the Bronx, to Romie and Maria's apartment on Sherman Avenue and East 167th Street.

RICO GOT OUT of his car, locked the doors, and armed the alarm. He walked over to the black SUV. The back door opened a crack. Rico grabbed the handle and opened the door fully then got in.

"Uncle Sal."

"Hey kid."

They embraced for a moment. Rico sat in a seat next to Uncle Sal facing the front of the SUV and nodded acknowledgement toward the two huge bodies in the front seat.

Salvatore Tattaglia was a well-respected New York mobster also known as 'The Bank'. He had an uncanny talent for math, envied by many a mathematician. Although not formally educated or trained, he had a gift and memory for numbers that became legendary. He would take customers' money and bets, never writing down anything and never getting anything wrong. Winners were paid their correct earnings and a complaint was never heard about miscalculations or errors. The bosses loved it mainly because there were no trails of incriminating evidence. Considered by many to have the Midas Touch, he started off in the numbers running racket, but it quickly became apparent to those in power that his talents could/should be utilized elsewhere. Over the next decade he studied the stock market, and the real estate industry, and made hundreds of millions of dollars for the mob in legitimate investments, with illegal mob laundered money. In an era where the mob invested in the stock market on Wall Street, legally owned prime real estate, ran dozens of legitimate businesses including restaurants and night clubs in the New York tri-state region, Sal the Bank was considered the unofficial CFO, Chief Financial Officer, for the portion of New York family run by Tony G.

Now in his late fifties, he had paid his dues and showed his loyalty to the mob by doing grunt work when he was in his twenties. Grunt work meant working as a muscle or enforcer or bodyguard; it meant doing robberies and it also meant executions of mob enemies. He didn't shy away from any of it, and rather enjoyed it. Although over the last fifteen or twenty years his primary obligation to the mob and Tony G was to be Sal the Bank, he still enjoyed going along with the boys for an occasional muscle job.

He studied the young man in front of him, remembering his days as an enforcer and muscle in his youth alongside Rico's father, Frederico Sr. 'Freddie' was Sal's best friend at the time. He kept a watchful distant eye on Frederico Jr., 'Rico', and made it his business to be there for the kid whenever he needed fatherly guidance, whether it be in the form of advice or money or muscle. He kept an eye on him while Rico was in prison through his contacts who were also doing time. He was pleased at Rico's growth into manhood and felt that Freddie would be pleased also. Rico was a sharp minded kid, wasn't afraid of hard work, had a strong character and wasn't into heavy drugs or drinking.

"Uncle Sal, I hate to bother you for petty non-sense."

"Rico, it's not a bother and let me be the judge of whether it's petty. I enjoy whenever I get a chance to see you," said Sal after exhaling cigar smoke toward the partially open window.

Rico felt stressed and lit a cigarette. "Thanks, Uncle Sal. I enjoy seeing you too and I'm really sorry we don't spend more time together. But today I reached out to you because I have a situation developing that is probably gonna get very explosive and I need two things. First, your advice and second, your promise that you won't interfere until I ask you."

CHAPTER

13

WHEN DEXTER ARRIVED at Maria and Roman's small apartment, a few members of their family were there consoling her and each other. The atmosphere in the apartment, as expected, was one of grief, agony and pain. They were preparing themselves to drive her to New Jersey to identify the body. Dexter hung around for a little while to pay his respects and to see Maria, then left walking down the three flights of stairs from their apartment. He was still numb and in shock. As he exited the building he heard Maria's voice calling his name. He looked up to see her at her window, waving for him to come back upstairs.

Maria met him on the second floor hallway landing. "Here Dex, this is the cell phone that he was using. He forgot it the day he went to New Jersey. Maybe you can use it to call his friends on the job and let them know what happened, okay?"

"Sure, okay. I'll work on it."

She called later thanking him for coming over and gave him the police's version of the facts. She wasn't sure about the arrangements yet, and would call him later when they were determined. She became emotional and began sobbing over the phone. Dexter suspected that, among other things, there was a financial issue, unsure that Roman had any type of life insurance coverage. He assured her that he would let Romie's friends at the job know.

"BOB, IT'S DEXTER REED. Listen, I'm calling to advise you that Roman Reyes was found dead in New Jersey. Can you please post something to inform his friends and co-workers at the company of this tragic occurrence? The funeral arrangements dates are yet to be determined. I will advise you when I know."

"Another thing, I'm gonna need a few days off. I'll let you know how many."

Next, Dexter called Josette. "Hey Jo, I just got some bad news. Roman was found shot dead in New Jersey. I'm going to be late for dinner at your place tonight. Yeah, I'm fine. Just gotta think some things through. I'll call you later."

Dexter hung up the phone and sat under the shade of a large elm tree at Mololy's Park. He came here sometimes on weekends for good basketball games with good players, but also came here during moments of reflection and meditation, for the peace and solitude that he found under a section of trees in the backdrop of the basketball courts.

It had been over forty-eight hours since the news of Roman's death, but Dexter was still emotionally paralyzed. He had made up his mind to go the IG's office and admit what little he knew, even if it meant that there would be a penalty to pay. He was staring down the barrel of a shotgun. He would probably lose his EMT card, forfeit his dream and chance to become a NYS paramedic, lose his job, and either get hit with a small fine or some jail time.

It didn't matter though; whoever did this to Roman had to pay, even if he, Dexter, had to suffer. Although he felt he did no wrong, he would sacrifice his freedom and go to jail, to do the right thing for Romie.

This situation caused Dexter to do some serious introspection and self-analysis. He considered himself a balanced and cool brother, and was described by many as an even-tempered individual who rarely got angry. He stayed in the middle of debates by others, never really feeling strongly toward either side of an argument, but able to see both sides.

Roman was different from Dexter. When he felt strongly about something he voiced his feelings. He wasn't worried about offending anyone and was ready to argue or debate his feelings to the point of throwing blows if it got that far. Dexter partially admired that about Roman and now felt that he had to adopt some of that philosophy or behavior for himself.

The Roman situation was totally different. It struck a strong chord in him. It struck his heartstrings, it struck home. There could be no shrugging the shoulders and moving on. There could be no indifference. There could be no repressing his anger. It was time to get furious and explode. He was going to have to reach out to his youngest brother, Miles, and incorporate his underground associates, because another compounding issue was that he still hadn't figured out whether he was a target of the law firm.

As Dexter sat in his car later that afternoon, it dawned on him to look into Roman's disposable phone for some answers. As soon as he opened it up, the name "Rico" popped up.
Dexter hit the call button and waited.

"Who's this?" answered the voice on the other end.

"This is Dexter, Roman's boy. You and me got problems."

Pause. "Listen, we can't talk on this phone. Meet me at the Bronx Zoo on Southern and 188 Street in thirty minutes," then he hung up.

The question of whether he was a target was still unanswered, however he didn't have time to gather Miles and his troops. Besides, Rico's voice didn't sound like a predator; it sounded more like someone who was on guard. He decided to meet him, hoping for a one on one meeting between the two of them, where he could bust up Rico before he went to the IG.

As he pulled up to the curb, he glanced around and saw a young white guy sitting parked in a BMW a few cars ahead. He looked like the same guy that he saw Roman talking to at the scene of a few car accidents, except that it was daylight and he had on sunglasses.

Dexter got out of his car quickly, thinking that Rico hadn't seen him yet, and he had the element of surprise. He picked up his pace, but Rico spotted him and stepped out of the car. Just what Dexter wanted; thoughts of just bum-rushing the little white guy responsible for Roman's death quickened his heartbeat and his pace. He charged at Rico and threw a right hand punch from his roots somewhere in Africa. The intensity on his face must have been evident, along with the fact that he telegraphed the punch, because Rico easily blocked the punch and shoved Dexter face down into the hood of the car, then stepped back.

Rico shook his head 'no' and momentarily lifted his sports jacket, exposing the handle of an automatic gun in Rico's waistband, as Dexter turned around and started to resume his attack.

Without hesitation or fear, Dexter threw another right hand at Rico's head, which partially caught a surprised Rico and glanced off his temple. Rico retaliated with a powerful left that caught Dexter in the right rib cage, causing him to drop his hands, followed by a right to Dexter's jaw that knocked him backward onto the BMW. He braced for the impact onto the hood of the car and prepared to bounce back at Rico, but the screeching of tires stopping right in front of him ceased the aggressions.

Two men got out of the car and pinned Dexter face down on the hood of the BMW.

"You move nigger, and I will chop you up and make you worm food," said one of them as he quickly zip-tied Dexter's wrists.

Rico looked around to make sure the commotion hadn't attracted the attention of police. The two musclemen stood Dexter up, facing Rico, who put his hand on the gun handle and repositioned it comfortably in his waistband.

"You got the wrong idea," said Rico. "I had nothing to do with Roman's death."

"Roman had a saying," replied Dexter, "he would say, 'you're bob-ing me,' as in giving me a B-O-B, 'bag of bullshit'. You're full of shit, man. Put the gun away, lose the gorillas, and we can finish this."

"Ain't happening today, brother. Maybe another day you and I can go a few rounds."

"Is that the same gun you shot Roman with?"

"Listen, brother, if you can put a lid on that anger for a minute, then we can talk. I'll tell you who killed Roman, but we can't stay here. Let's take a drive and talk."

Dexter noticed Rico glance around occasionally as he spoke and got the impression that Rico wasn't a predator, but a prey. Although, a prey with a gun and bodyguards.

Rico nodded toward the passenger side of the BMW and told Dexter "get in."

As they drove off Rico said, "Look man, I'm not trying to hurt you or anybody, otherwise you'd be dead by now.

The guy who killed Roman is after me too." Rico watched in the rear-view mirror as the tail that his Uncle Sal forced him to take pulled out from the curb half a block back and followed at a discreet distance.

"Who killed Roman?"

"The lawyer I work for had Roman hit because he was talking about squealing and he wanted 'quiet money' to shut up. In essence, he tried to blackmail the lawyer. Roman was a goldfish trying to outmuscle a shark. I had no idea what was going down until it happened."

Some of Rico's words about Roman were true, Dexter could attest to that. "So, who is this lawyer, and is he after me?"

Rico drove down Fordham Road and turned into the Fordham University parking lot, talking as he drove. He pulled into a desolate section of the parking lot and cut Dexter's plastic hand-cuffs. He explained about his involvement with the law firm and the ruthlessness of Spellman.

"So what happens now?" asked Dexter.

"When you called me you used Roman's phone right? "

"So what?"

"The only reason I answered was because I knew it was Roman's phone and he was dead. I'm asking you to hold on to it as insurance, in case anything happens to me. In its memory, it has all of the calls Roman made from the scene of accidents to me and it was bugged so the attorney could monitor it. He can't claim that he had no knowledge of the activity and throw me under the bus. I worked for Spellman so that implicates him."

"I knew the law firm was involved somehow and I was going to the Inspector General as a witness, to give testimony against the law firm, when I called you," said Dexter.

"Do me a favor and hold off for a day or two. Let me think this out and how I'm gonna play this," said Rico as he watched the tail pull into a parking spot one row over.

DEXTER DROVE TO HIS apartment contemplating the new revelation regarding Roman's death. Should he believe and trust Rico, or should he go to the police and IG with the story? He really had no significant evidence to give them and wondered if it was worth saying anything, just yet.

He opened the door to his apartment and went to the kitchen. He wasn't a heavy alcohol drinker, but he had a few assorted bottles on top of his fridge. He felt like today was one of those days when he needed a stiff drink. He reached past the bottles of Red Wine, Rum and Liqueur, then took an unopened bottle of Jameson Irish whiskey, a birthday gift from an Irish buddy from last year. He poured a half glass and walked to his couch, but before he sat down he reached over to the CD player and turned it on. He had an old Stanley Turrentine disc loaded on the player and it began playing a soulful jazz tune with Stanley's rich tenor sax belting out a powerful riff. He sat down and took a swig of the Jameson's. It warmed his throat and chest as it went down.

He realized he should call Josette and cancel dinner with her tonight at her place. She would understand, he was certain. She might even rush over to comfort him and be with him. That might not be such a bad thing, come to think about it, he thought, as he took another swig of Jameson.

"Hey Jo, I'm home. I'm not going to make it tonight."

"Are you okay, Dex? Did you eat something?"

"Nah, I didn't eat anything yet. Maybe later, not hungry now."

"Listen, I'm coming over. I'll bring you some fish and a salad, okay?"

"Okay, baby. Sounds good, thanks."

That was easy, he thought.

But the sorrow, or the Jameson, was taking over his heart now. They had killed Romie, his boy, his best friend, his brother, and they had a stranger, Rico, looking over his shoulder. This law firm seemed to have some sinister cloud over to them, where death seemed to lurk in their shadow. But Rico said a name, what was it? Spellman. Dexter got up and made his way to the table in the kitchen. He pulled out his laptop and put it on the table, then began doing a web search of attorneys named Spellman in the Bronx. He wanted to have a face to depict his anger and hatred. His heart ached over the loss of Roman and the effect it would have on Roman's family, especially his wife and RayRay.

RICO LAYED IN Eve's king-sized bed, staring at the ceiling as she lay naked and asleep, with her head on his chest. They had gone out to dinner at a nice Manhattan restaurant where he tried to console her. He picked up the tab, never mentioning the whole evening that he had any knowledge or details of Roman's death. Afterwards they came to her apartment and he continued to console her, unsure if he should attempt any sexual overtures. To his surprise, she was the sexual aggressor, and they had buck wild, crazy, passionate sex. At first she was listless and hesitant, but after a while became more involved. Rico realized that she was using sex as a powerful release.

Things between them were not quite resolved but the sex was still *off the chain*. He had begun to notice a pattern of bi-polar type behavior where she seemed to alternate between Eve the Wonderful, and Evil-lyn the Wicked Witch of the West. At first he thought there was a correlation with her menstrual cycle, but later dismissed that idea and since the sex was so damn good, he put up with it. She put such a high level of intensity and energy into the sex, without any restrictions, that every session was a marathon. It had been Rico's experience that some women often had lists of things that they declared they don't and won't do during sex. Eve had no such list. Neither did Rico. She did whatever Rico wanted and did it with feverish delight, as if her only goal was to make him climax. That, and her gorgeous looks and body, kept him coming back.

As he lay there, his mind went to the Spellman situation. He felt comfortable that he was prepared for Spellman's next move, whatever it may be. He was going to meet with him today as usual for their weekly case file review. Rico had gone to work after he heard of Roman's death as if nothing happened. In their few short interactions since then, Spellman only spoke about law firm business and nothing else, with a tone that was cold, business-like and impersonal.

He planned to put Spellman on notice and warn him tomorrow that if anything like what happened to Roman should happen to him or his family, there would be a contract out on Spellman's life that no body-guards would be able to stop.

He looked at the night table alarm clock that read 4:11am. He eased away from Eve and grabbed his clothes from the bed foot-bench. He had to go back to his apartment, shower, shave and get clean clothes for work later that morning.

He knelt on the bed, brushed Eve's long black hair away from face and kissed her lips. She smiled.

"Eve, I'm gonna go. Got stuff to do early in the morning."

"Okay, Rico but come back to bed for a quickie."

"You know our quickies can last a coupla hours," said Rico laughing, then he smacked her on the ass firmly, the loud clap echoing thru the bedroom. She smiled again.

Rico dressed and put the new 9-mm Glock in his pants waistband. He took the elevator down, paused at the lobby door and calmly looked both ways. Upon seeing no pedestrian traffic on the sidewalk, he walked out into the night. As he walked to his car he was on high alert, but he felt comfortable being on alert. Prison, where one had to be constantly on alert, had prepped him for this. For a carton of cigarettes, one's best friend could sell you out or set you up to be shanked by an enemy with a make-shift knife. Many inmates were stabbed in the back, or had faces or throats cut, because a 'buddy' had distracted them while an enemy snuck up on them and quick-shanked them, then walked calmly away as if nothing happened.

He watched the few cabs and bits of traffic as they traveled on the street, paying attention to drivers and passengers. A few minutes later he reached his car and got in, unaware of the male observing him, sitting in a parked car ten cars behind him near the corner intersection. Rico started his car and put on a music CD, then lit a cigarette. He saw a man walking down the block from behind him and gently pulled the Glock from his waistband, resting it on his thigh, covered by his sport coat. His footsteps grew louder in the still of the night as he got closer to the car. Rico coolly watched him through his driver's side mirror while puffing on his cigarette, also looking to see if he had a partner mirroring him across the street, but the lighting was poor and there were shadows everywhere.

As the individual passed under a street lamp Rico was able to get a glimpse of a face through the car mirror. A crack-head, thought Rico, in tattered jeans and a worn tee shirt as he passed the car, oblivious of Rico taking another drag on his cigarette, his hand still on the Glock. The crack-head disappeared down the street and into the shadows of the night.

Rico took one final drag, then flipped the half spent cigarette out the window of the car and pulled off from the curb, putting the piece back in his pants waistband. His headlights lit up the two-lane street for about one hundred feet in front of him. He noticed as he got to the corner, a parked car pulled out about half a block from where he had just left. Odd, he thought, he hadn't noticed anybody walking to any cars on that street for the few minutes while he took that smoke and he had sent Uncle Sal's tail home when he got to Eve's. Had Uncle Sal sent them back?

He turned at the traffic light heading toward the highway, leaving the exclusive section of Riverdale and toward his apartment in the North Bronx. In his rearview mirror he spotted headlights about half a block back turning toward the highway also, apparently keeping a distance to avoid detection. Spellman's attempt to monitor his movements, wondered Rico?

Suddenly, a loud explosion echoed off every building on that city block and Rico's car became a rolling fireball. The explosion caused glass to shatter from nearby windows and storefronts. Rico's body was thrown from the car during the blast and he lay twisted face down on the street bloodied, smoldering, and motionless. The carcass of the car lit up the night like a campfire in the woods, with the smoke rising toward the blackened sky and the smell of gasoline and burnt plastic permeating the scene.

The car belonging to the headlights following Rico slowly pulled up to the scene. The black Ford Crown Vic slowed down near Rico's body and the driver peered down. The driver tossed the detonator in his hand onto the empty front passenger's seat, then got out of the car.

Clean-shaven with a military crew cut, he had a section of burned skin at his right temple area, which he suffered during one of many tours in the Middle East. He pulled the collar of his jacket up to partially cover his face and looked quickly to see if anyone was around.

As he walked toward the body, Rico suddenly groaned and tried to turn over on his back. The driver of the car pulled out his handgun, kicked Rico forcefully in the chest, forcing him onto his back and effortlessly pumped three bullets into Rico's chest, center mass, intending for each bullet to hit a chamber of the heart. Rico's smoldering body jerked from the impact of each bullet. The shooter tugged at his jacket collar and kept his face partially hidden, keeping his head down toward the ground to prevent a frontal view of his face for witnesses or security cameras, and got back in his car. He avoided looking up at the nearby apartment windows. As he drove past the responding New York City Fire Department trucks a few blocks away, he made a phone call, "It's done. Yes, I'm sure. He's definitely dead."

The fire trucks stopped and the fire crews jumped off grabbing their equipment. One of the firemen stopped when he noticed Rico's body and yelled, "Hey Lou, there's a body over here!"

Another fireman closer to the body walked over and bent down, taking off his heavy gloves he felt for a pulse and excitedly proclaimed, "Lou, the poor bastard's got a pulse."

The fire lieutenant got on the radio and directed the dispatcher to expedite the ambulance, while giving directions to his crews on controlling the car fire. The BMW had rolled into a parked car and began to set the second car ablaze, but the fire crews made little work of controlling and extinguishing the fires.

One of the two firemen near Rico began cutting his clothing before attempting to pull them off when he noticed two strange things: there was a gun in the waistband of the burnt guy's pants and he was wearing a bullet-proof vest.

The police department arrived a few minutes later and began to rope off and barricade the scene, followed by the arrival of the ambulance. The ambulance crew checked for pulses, applied oxygen and immediately began spinal immobilization of Rico. In the ambulance they finished cutting off his clothes, took off the bullet-proof vest and checked for further injuries.

"HEY SAL, YOU GOT A CALL," said one of the heavily muscled bodyguards handing the cell phone to him.

"Who is it?"

"One of our NYPD moles," said the bodyguard.

Sal took the phone and spoke into it, "Make it short and sweet."

"It's 'X-Man'. I just got word from a buddy in a north Bronx precinct that there was a crash and explosion last night, early this morning. The driver is listed in serious condition, but he is alive. The car was registered to your nephew Frederico. The detectives and fire inspectors there are considering it suspicious."

"Awright, X-Man. What hospital is the driver at? South Bronx Mercy? Good work. Keep me posted on any further developments. Hold on..." and Sal handed the phone back to Enzo, who was waiting. Sal nodded to Enzo, "here, kiss X-man with double the usual amount and tell him I am pleased with the info, then have the guys bring the car around. We're going to the hospital."

Sal walked to his office and shut the door. He got on the phone and made several calls, setting a series of events into motion.

AS SAL ENTERED THE hospital elevator, he thought about another time and another hospital visit. While the elevator ascended to the eighth floor, he recalled a scene from twenty years ago.

"Hey Freddie, whatcha doin' tonight after we do this job? Wanna join the card game at Gino's? You know there's always big money on the table at his place."

"C'mon Sal, I ain't stupid. That's like you getting in the ring with me. You and the cards talk to each other, you know who has what cards as soon as they're dealt. You tryin' to take bread out of my kids mouth?" asked Freddie.

"I don't talk to the cards, I just know the law of probability, or averages. I would never take dough from you. We always split our winnings. Besides, your son is my son. Rico is gonna marry my little girl, Annette, when they grow up and be my son-in-law."

They both chuckled, as the driver of the car eased to stop. They were on a hit job that night. The hit was on an opposing crime-family member and it was ordered by Tony G. They were going to make the hit when the mark arrived home, which according to their informants was approximately 11pm every night.

They sat in their car, awaiting their targets arrival, when another sedan drove by them. The sedan, a black Lincoln Continental, slowed down as it neared the car Sal and Freddie were in, then sped past them, making a u-turn at the corner, one hundred feet away. The Lincoln then slowly drove back toward their car.

"Look out," yelled Freddie, as he raised his handgun.

The target was in the Lincoln with two bodyguards and the driver, each with a raised handgun. Freddie had sensed that something was amiss when the Lincoln u-turned at the corner and was the first to fire. His first two shots caught the target in the head and throat, then began the return volley from the Lincoln, as Sal and their driver returned several shots at the Lincoln. The noise from the firing of several guns almost simultaneously, sounded like Fourth of July fireworks. Both cars were pointing in opposite directions, as their occupants waged a lead-spitting war from less than twenty feet away from each other.

"Let's get outta here," said Freddie to the driver, tapping the back of the driver's seat forcefully. The driver grunted and floored the gas pedal. "Sal, you okay?" asked Freddie, turning around to visually examine Sal.

Sal was holding his right shoulder. "I guess you'll have to call me 'lefty' now," he said. The blood oozed between his fingers from the entry wound of the bullet. Sal looked up from the bloody mess that was his shoulder and froze in shock. Freddie was bleeding from four different areas of his chest. He had been in the direct line of fire, seated behind the driver's seat, directly facing the shooters in the Lincoln. The car door had taken many of the bullets meant for them, but some had found their mark, probably a few of them were meant for Sal but Freddie was in the way. Freddie, whose only concern was about his buddy Sal, showed no pain or discomfort at first, but his skin color seemed pale to Sal, even in the backseat of an unlit car at night.

Sal looked up front to the driver, who seemed to have tied a rag around his bloodied hand and drove in a hurried pace away from the area. The windshield had several cracks and spider-webs on it from the shootout, as did the mirrors.

"Head to the hospital. Bronx Mercy. I'll have someone meet us out front and take the guns and ammo."

Sal turned his attention back to Freddie, who had slumped on his side, his head inches away from Sal's thigh. Through labored and gurgled breathing, he was saying something. Sal leaned on his elbow and put his ear next to Freddie's mouth. "What did you say, Freddie?"

"Take care of my familia..."

Freddie died in the operating room that night as Sal sat outside the room. When one of the doctors came out to notify the family of the pronouncement of Freddie's death, Sal was the only one there. He knew before they reached the hospital that Freddie's death was imminent and that it was part of the lifestyle they lived, but it still was a devastating blow. Although he picked up on the doctor's unsympathetic 'you Italian gangster guys' demeanor, he dismissed the doctor's attitude as he tried valiantly to maintain emotional control. He was glad that no one else was around to see him bawling like a baby later.

AS THEY LEFT the elevator, Sal walked toward the nurse's station, where a few nurses and a doctor in an operating scrub suit were talking.

"Hello, nurse. I'm here for one of your patients, Frederico Lavore Jr."

The nurses and the doctor all stopped their conversation in unison and looked up at Sal. He knew right away what that meant.

"Okay, sir. Are you a member of the family?"

"Yes, I'm his uncle."

The doctor stepped forward, "Hello, sir. My name is Dr. Bannerman. Please follow me, there is a private room right over here where we can talk."

"What is your name, sir?"

"Just call me Sal, doc, and I'd appreciate it if we just cut to the chase."

"Okay, Sal. I'm sorry to tell you this, but your nephew passed away on the operating table thirty minutes ago due to massive traumatic head injuries sustained in a car explosion. We tried a few procedures to mitigate the brain damage but it was without success. He was in tremendous physical shape and that helped him last as long as it did, but the head trauma was just too much. Again, I'm sorry to have to give you this news and I offer my condolences to you and your family. Unless you have any questions, I'm going to give you a few minutes alone, then send the nurse in to get some of your nephew's information."

CHAPTER

14

STEVEN SPELLMAN HUNG up the phone. The time on the alarm clock read 5:11am on the night table as he sat up in bed. One headache taken care of, he thought, as he looked over at his wife, who lay in bed next to him asleep, in a white satin baby-doll two-piece. The realization of ridding himself of the last annoying and potentially problematic obstacle gave him a sense of relief. As he sat there in boxer shorts, he wrestled with the urge to undress Michelle and make love to her, but she didn't like unplanned sex lately and usually put up a fierce resistance, which aggravated him to no end. Instead, he decided, he would get up and go by his mistress for a couple of hours, before going to the office.

He paid for her apartment; and the arrangement was that he would stop by anytime, with a courtesy phone call ahead of time to allow her to get rid of any visitors before he got there. He decreased his visits to her when he began to have irregular heartbeats and take meds for the condition, but the reality was that he felt better after a session with her than at any other time.

Spellman washed and dressed hurriedly in his bathroom, then walked past Michelle's huge walk-in closet and wrote a quick note that he put on the mirror in her bathroom. The spacious home was dark and quiet, the service staff had yet to arrive, as Spellman descended the winding staircase to the garage entry-door in the kitchen. He punched in the security code to disarm the door, then walked out into the three-car garage.

The motion lights clicked on as soon as he stepped down the three stairs into the garage. He walked past his pride and joy, a silver Bugatti that gleamed under the lights, and past Michelle's Jaguar before getting into his 'everyday' Jag.

He pulled out of the garage, passed his back-up Range Rover parked outside the garage, and down the long driveway off the property onto the street. He proceeded to the intersection where he came upon a disabled Benz with flashers on and hood up, partially blocking his way. The driver of the car, a thickly built man dressed in a black trench coat, dark trousers and a small brimmed hat, walked over toward Spellman, who rolled down his driver's window.

"Hi, neighbor. Do you need me to call a tow for you?" asked Spellman.

The man reached into the car and forcefully opened the door, to Spellman's surprise.

"What the ...," Spellman suddenly realized that another man was opening the passenger side door and that the first guy must have hit the unlock button. Before he could open his mouth to offer money, he was punched in the face by both men. He slumped like a sack of potatoes into the leather and wood-grained console beside him. The two strong men easily lifted him and pushed him to the floor of the backseat. One of them grabbed his cell phone.

The first man went back to his car and lowered the raised hood, he then put Spellman's cell phone under the front tire of his car and drove off, smashing the phone, followed by Spellman's Jaguar closely behind, driven by his partner.

When Steven Spellman awoke, he had a splitting headache and his right jaw was swollen and throbbing. His mouth felt like sandpaper and he became aware that something was in it. He tried to spit it out, then force it out with his tongue, but certain movements made his jaw hurt even more. He tried to move his hands and became cognizant of the fact that his hands and legs were zip-tied to the heavy wooden chair, along with his torso being tied by a thick rope to the chair.

He looked around and saw that he was in some kind of warehouse. He saw his Jaguar parked about a hundred feet away from him. As his mind cleared he looked around to survey his surroundings. Although the lighting was dim, he could make out that there were several other cars, in different stages of repair, placed in an organized manner around the warehouse. Each car had a tiered toolbox next to it. He realized he was in some kind of auto mechanics garage, but nobody seemed to be around.

He flexed his hand and tried to move it freely, but it was securely bound to the chair. There was no slack and he was even beginning to feel a slight numbness in his hands, due to the tightness of the plastic zip ties. His jaw was throbbing fiercely and he figured it was probably broken during the ambush.

Who were these guys and what did they want, he wondered. Was this a kidnapping and ransom situation? Who was behind this? Could Michelle have orchestrated this? And if she didn't, then who? Would they kill him even if they got their money, since he saw the faces of the two gorillas that grabbed him? Wild thoughts ran through his mind.

The sound of a slammed door in a distance behind him brought his focus back to his surroundings. He could hear footsteps and the voices of at least two men walking toward him. As they came around in front of him, it was three men, two of which were the ones that kidnapped him. Through the gag that was in his mouth, he started making sounds to let them know that he wanted to talk, but the pain in his jaw increased tenfold when he moved it.

"Save your energy, asshole," said one of the group, "you're gonna need it in a few minutes," as he approached Spellman with a knife. Spellman's eyes became two blood-shot baseballs when he saw the knife approaching. He was helpless, he couldn't say or do anything. The not being able to *say* anything was more alarming for Spellman; who always felt that he could talk or bullshit his way out of any situation, and then manipulate the law to buttress his position.

The knife was placed on the right side of his neck and held there, "After what you did to Rico, I'm gonna enjoy playing with you later," smiled the knife-wielder, who took the knife and started cutting Spellman's tie and shirt. He then ripped off the tie, sleeves and rest of the shirt, exposing Spellman's bare upper body.

Spellman felt relief that he wasn't gutted right there, but his fears were further heightened as the realization hit him that this wasn't a kidnapping for ransom. This was revenge. At that moment, he became aware of a sharp aching pain in his mid-chest radiating up to his shoulder and jaw. The crushing, squeezing pain was all too familiar to Spellman, it was the same pain as first heart attack, a year ago. This time it was much more severe. He wasn't sure which hurt more, the pain in his chest or the pain in his probably, broken jaw.

The second man had taken the cap off of a needle and syringe, pressed down to let out a little of a clear viscous solution, and approached Spellman. Spellman felt sweat trickling down his face and dripping onto his chest. As he looked down at the beads of sweat, he saw his apical pulse on his chest where his heart appeared to be beating a million times a minute, and realized that his breathing rate had tripled.

The second man, dressed in a cheap gray plaid suit, tied a thin twelve-inch long rubber tubing tightly around Spellman's right upper arm, which caused his veins to become engorged and prominent.

Spellman groaned through the gag and his body began seizing just as the needle was about to be injected into his vein. His assailant with needle paused, and backed up, watching Spellman's seizing. His whole body was twitching vigorously and his arms, legs began to spasm uncontrollably. The puddle under the chair was evidence that he lost control of his bladder.

"Did you give him the drugs already?" asked one of the abductors.

"Nah, he's having some kinda seizure. Maybe he's got some kind of seizure history."

Suddenly Spellman stopped seizing. His body went limp and his head slumped into his chest.

"What the fuck is going on? This guy is so pale he looks like a ghost and now his lips are turning blue. Is this legit or is he acting out?" asked the other abductor.

"This motherfucka is dying," said the gray suit after putting the syringe down and checking for a pulse. "He literally must have had the crap scared out of him. He had a heart attack before I could load him up with the drugs. Call Sal and let him know. See what he wants us to do with this guy."

DEXTER WENT TO his mailbox and retrieved his mail on his way to his car. Walking to his car he sorted through the mail, putting the bills to the back of the stack. Something caught his eye in the half dozen envelopes, but before he could take it out, a stocky white guy in dark slacks and navy sports coat suddenly stepped in front of him impeding his way. Dexter had momentarily dropped his guard and allowed himself to be cornered, now another stocky white guy was standing behind him. Both men were shorter than him, but appeared to be bodybuilders or weight lifters with huge massive necks, chests and shoulders, and both were in the two hundred fifty pound plus class. Both were deadly serious with business-like matter of fact expressions on their faces. The one in front of him motioned toward a parked black SUV where an imposing figure sat in the back seat puffing on a thick Cuban cigar.

"I don't wanna hurt ya kid. I'm here to talk and extend an olive branch as a favor to my nephew. Don't piss me off, just get in the car," said the large man in a voice that was both a request and a demand. "Please."

Dexter looked around. Nobody else was in the car and the two bodyguard types were standing only a few feet away and seemed poised to pick him up and throw him in the back seat if he balked. But Dexter wasn't going to run. He was tired of looking over his shoulder and for some reason felt that the three gorillas weren't there to hurt him.

The man in the back seat put up his hand to stop Dexter, "You got a piece on you?"

Dexter shook his head.

"Then you don't mind if we check you…"

Both bodyguards closed in, one patted him down, then nodded to the back seat.

Dexter got in the SUV. The two gorillas closed the door and got in the front seat of the Cadillac Escalade. "Enzo, drive around for a while so we can talk," said the older man to the driver. The SUV then drove off slowly. The tinted back windows kept the atmosphere dark and somber. The man in the back seat studied Dexter, as Dexter watched him. He saw an Italian 'man of the belly', in the old Sicilian tradition. The two body-guards unquestioning obedience towards the Italian man, revered figurative belly power, and literal belly, manifested in physical midsection girth.

He had the requisite jowls and a double chin that hung over an opened-collar white button-up shirt and dark plaid sports jacket. His eyes were piercing, staring, reading Dexter like they were reading lines of a book.

Finally the big man spoke, "Please forgive me for being short with you, I am grieving for a family member. My nephew set things up so that I was his insurance policy. He told me about his involvement with the law firm and the problems that developed. He asked me to handle a few things in the event something happened to him. One of the things he asked me to handle was his remorse for you and your partner. He asked me to give you fifty thousand dollars and asked that you give it to the family of your partner, who left a wife and kids. It certainly can't replace him, but surely the wife can find some way to put fifty grand to use for the household," he handed Dexter an envelope with what felt like cash.

"Also, he asked me to give you twenty five thousand dollars for what you have gone through over the past month," and he handed Dexter another smaller envelope apparently also filled with money.

Dexter didn't reach to accept the second envelope.

"This is not dirty money, blood money or drug money, if that's what you're thinking. It's not from a bank robbery either and it can't be traced back to you. This is actual life insurance money that comes from a half million-dollar life insurance policy that he took out once he started having good paydays. Most of it goes to his mother and some family members. Some to you and your dead partner's family. My nephew was a big hearted kid and a smart kid," said Uncle Sal as he forcefully pushed the second envelope into Dexter's hand.

"I didn't realize that Rico was dead. I don't know what to say, except I'm sorry for your loss and am grateful for Rico's generosity. Thank you for delivering it. What is going to happen with the lawyer?"

"You seem to be a smart kid. You figured out that the lawyer was behind it all and probably wondered if he would eventually come after you. My nephew left incriminating evidence for the IG's Office that implicates the lawyer in the ambulance chasing and insurance scam. He also left evidence for the feds of insider trading. The icing on the cake is that an anonymous tip was conveyed to NYPD of a significant stash of cocaine and cash in his office. The police will arrest him today as soon as he pulls into his office. They will find a sizeable amount of cocaine hidden in his office closet, courtesy of Rico's knowledge of the security system and codes. The police will follow protocol and test him, and Spellman will test positive for cocaine in his system, courtesy of a visit by a couple of my boys to the lawyer on his way to work.

My nephew didn't want him killed. He felt that for someone like that, it was more about him suffering the public shame, humiliation and disbarment. It would be more hurtful for him to suffer the loss of his money, homes, cars and his freedom. Rico felt that he would commit suicide in jail within a few months anyway.

I am going to personally add to his stress and jail woes. I have connections in just about every jail in New York. I will make sure that he will be repeatedly beat up, raped and shanked. I will make his stay in prison a living hell.

All I can tell you, and all you need to know, is that he will be paid back in full for what he did to my nephew and others. He will never bother anyone again. You have my word that you don't have to worry about him."

The black SUV dropped Dexter off at the street where his car was parked, near his apartment. There was no exchange of formalities or pleasantries. The bodyguards opened the door, Dexter got out and everyone went about their business.

He got in his car and turned on the radio looking to hear some soothing jazz while he sat back and tried to absorb what had just happened: his abduction; learning of Rico's death; the receipt of the generous cash gift for Maria; the receipt of cash for himself; and the revelation of Spellman's probable future. Instead of music he got *the news*. The newscaster reported that millionaire attorney Steven Spellman was under arrest in a NYC hospital after NYPD found a cache of drugs and money in his car and office. The newscaster mentioned that Spellman was being investigated by the Inspector General's Office and questioned by NYPD about involvement in the murder of another person involved in the same investigation. There was some speculation that he may have been preparing to flee town under the pressure of the investigation.

Dexter knew that Spellman was under pressure from at least three law enforcement agencies and wasn't the least bit concerned with Dexter.

As he sat there he suddenly remembered that there was something in the mail that caught his eye. He flipped through the mail, then *saw it.* An envelope from the New York State Department of Health, his heart started racing. He opened it. It was a letter congratulating him on passing the New York State paramedic exam with a total score of ninety and becoming certified as a New York State paramedic.

In chasing his dream he had secured the first benchmark of that dream, he had attained his paramedic certification. However, he felt that he had to re-evaluate his goals. Medicine was no longer on a dreamy pedestal, the law had saved the day and he had become aware of the power of the legal system to effect massive change on the city, state and national level.

He wondered if it was wise to make any decisions at this point in time. But he realized that he needed to take a few days off and reassess everything. Hell, after what he'd been through, take the damn month off.

He felt bittersweet, conflicted feelings. He felt a little like celebrating, but there was also a little sadness. The celebratory feelings came from the fact that the person responsible for Roman's death would soon pay for his death. Also, even though dampened by the recent turn of events, he felt happy over getting the news that he passed the NYS paramedic exam.

The feelings of sadness and sorrow were lingering due to Roman's death and Dexter's attachment to RayRay. Dexter felt that the boy wouldn't understand his father's absence and wondered how he would handle it. Would RayRay even be aware of Roman's absence? And if so, how would a kid with autism express his heartache and sorrow? He knew that he would have to step up for RayRay and become an active part in his life. He felt comforted by the fact that his girlfriend, Josette, worked in this field and would be there for support to help him with navigating the road ahead, with regard to RayRay.

He needed some time off. Maybe he would take some of the money, grab Josette and go to the Caribbean for a week.

THE NEXT DAY Dexter took Maria to five banks to deposit the money. He told her it wasn't wise to keep the money in the apartment. He also told her, suddenly putting a large amount of money in the bank might draw attention from the bank and the government. Dexter gave Maria twenty thousand of his twenty-five thousand to go along with the fifty that Rico left her.

"Hey Maria, I want to ask you something," he said as he dropped her and the kids at the curb in front of their apartment building.

"Sure, Dex. Ask me anything."

"Do you mind if I take RayRay to the park today? And occasionally spend time with him and little Roman?"

"I would love for you to spend time with Ray and lil Roman."

"Good, then Ray and I are going to the park and grab something to eat right now. I'll bring him back in an hour or two."

"Fine," said Maria, who then took the hand of Roman Jr. and proceeded up the stairs toward the lobby door. She stopped at the door, turned and mouthed the words THANK YOU to Dexter. He smiled, took Ray's little hand and they walked to the park.

At the park, Dexter got on one knee. He began their traditional greeting by putting out his right hand, shoulder high and said "high five" and received a high five. "Low five," he said, and received a low five. "Bump," was the next step in the routine and he gently extended his fist forward and received a soft fist bump, then he said "kiss." They both leaned forward and kissed each other on the cheek. Dexter wrapped both arms around RayRay, hugging him, then stood up with the little boy in his arms. He was always amazed at how Ray performed their greeting routine, yet he couldn't say hello, good-by or his name. He took it to mean that Ray just needed special attention and therapy. Ray had a lot to share with the world and Dexter would do everything in his power to help him.

"You know Uncle Dex loves you, right?" he said while the little body squirmed to get down. He looked into Ray's eyes and saw some recognition and acceptance momentarily, but the boy's attention and gaze began jumping all over the park. He put him down and immediately Ray let out a squeal and took off full speed for the swings like a little bull.

Dexter grinned and took off after him in a light jog, becoming a chaser.

AUTHOR

Robert J. Little is a highly decorated, retired FDNY/EMS employee. Born, raised, educated and worked in the Bronx, New York, the author graduated from DeWitt Clinton High School, Mercy College, then earned a law degree from Rutgers University School of Law, Newark, New Jersey.

Robert worked for the New York City Emergency Medical Service, which later was merged with the Fire Department of New York City, for thirty-four years, in various titles that included motor vehicle operator, emergency medical technician, supervising emergency medical technician, paramedic and assistant manager. He has also worked for law firms in the Bronx and Westchester counties, in addition to the New York State Unified Court System.

He enjoys writing and is working on finishing his second EMS novel.

CPSIA information can be obtained at www.ICGtesting.com
Printed in the USA
BVOW02*2324040115

381667BV00002B/31/P